David McCaddon is an award-winning playwright and a published author of modern crime thrillers. He lives in Cheshire and before retiring in 2017 to concentrate on his writing, he was a seasoned IT consultant who had worked in computing for over 46 years and spent the past 34 years specialising in police systems. His extensive experience has involved him developing computer systems throughout a large number of the UK's police forces and worldwide including Australia, Hong Kong, Botswana, USA and Canada.

For my dear parents, Len and Nancy McCaddon.

David McCaddon

A QUESTION OF TIME

AUSTIN MACAULEY PUBLISHERS™
LONDON • CAMBRIDGE • NEW YORK • SHARJAH

Copyright © David McCaddon (2021)

The right of David McCaddon to be identified as author of this work has been asserted by the author in accordance with section 77 and 78 of the Copyright, Designs and Patents Act 1988.

All rights reserved. No part of this publication may be reproduced, stored in a retrieval system, or transmitted in any form or by any means, electronic, mechanical, photocopying, recording, or otherwise, without the prior permission of the publishers.

Any person who commits any unauthorised act in relation to this publication may be liable to criminal prosecution and civil claims for damages.

This is a work of fiction. Names, characters, businesses, places, events, locales, and incidents are either the products of the author's imagination or used in a fictitious manner. Any resemblance to actual persons, living or dead, or actual events is purely coincidental.

A CIP catalogue record for this title is available from the British Library.

ISBN 9781528997980 (Paperback)
ISBN 9781528997997 (ePub e-book)

www.austinmacauley.com

First Published (2021)
Austin Macauley Publishers Ltd
25 Canada Square
Canary Wharf
London
E14 5LQ

A Question of Time is a very different book from my previously published crime novels – *Following Digital Footprints, In Digital Pursuit* and *The Final Footprint*. It's set initially in North Wales and Chester in 1967. Whilst the book is of course purely fictional, I have fond memories of that time and I have appreciated the reminders of the area that I have received from a number of old and new friends in Buckley, North Wales.

I am especially appreciative of my family and friends with their ongoing encouragement and support. A huge thank you to Annabelle Hull who has helped me with my writing projects over the years both on and off stage and a special thank you to one of my fellow choristers, Andy Maxfield, whose input has also been very much appreciated.

Above all, thank you to my dear wife Joan, Simon, Karen and Jake for your understanding when I have disappeared for hours on end to work on the books.

Prologue

Chester
Saturday, 25th November 1967, 11.45pm

No one had seen him sneak into the alleyway, he'd made absolutely sure of that. To be honest he was well dressed for once and he looked ready for a good night out so no one would have possibly given him a second glance anyway. He'd even had time to have a shave and dab on some of that aftershave that he'd hardly used; the one that his dear old mother had bought him for Christmas a couple of years ago, just before she'd passed away. As he dabbed it on, he thought to himself, *In any case why should anyone notice me, they've never noticed me before.* He was right they'd never noticed him before and in fact he'd always felt he was ignored even throughout all of his school days right the way through from nursery.

He was the one who always seemed to be on his own in the corner of the playground; the one who was always last to be chosen for the football team or the one not even invited on the school trip. The one they picked on, the one who they had bullied time after time, the one they chose to have their head ducked in the school toilets. He had been so glad to leave school when he was fifteen and at least try and find his own way through life.

But for weeks now in his head he'd gone through the same routine. He'd sat in bed thinking it all through, over and over again. But tonight was different, much different, this was for real. Oh yes, this was the night, it had to be tonight, the night when all his careful and meticulous planning would be tested to the absolute limit.

After driving around the city centre to find somewhere suitable, he'd managed to park his old rusting Morris Minor car out of sight just down the road from the junction of Music Hall Passage with Leen Lane. He crouched down in the dimly lit alleyway just behind a large pile of discarded cardboard boxes where no one could possibly see him and he waited patiently. He looked anxiously at his watch again. It seemed as though he'd been there for hours. He could hear his heart beating faster than normal, almost racing at times. Minutes later the clock on the nearby cathedral chimed heralding in the Sunday morning and he knew that anytime now the crowds would be leaving the pubs and clubs in Northgate Street and beyond, laughing and joking as they headed for their various buses, trains and taxi journeys home.

Soon would come his big moment. This was it. He had planned it almost with military precision and knew that exactly thirty minutes later, once she had tidied up the bar area and locked up the club, she would head off to the taxi rank and take this same route, the same one she took every Saturday night without fail. He'd watched her for weeks now and he knew her every routine, you could even set your watch by her.

He could now hear the laughter and shouting from the last of the midnight revellers as they made their way home. He watched in disgust as one partygoer clearly the worse for wear took a slight detour and urinated against a brick wall just a few feet away from the side of him. Gradually the footsteps died away and suddenly it was all quiet again, it was so peaceful you could almost hear a pin drop. Then out of the darkness he could hear footsteps approaching, there was no mistaking it, stiletto heels picking their way over the uneven cobble stones.

He peeked out from behind the wall and there she stood on her own under a badly lit street light momentarily stopping to light up a cigarette. She stood for a brief moment and inhaled, relaxed for once after another hard night's work. A mixture of excitement and fear came over him.

It was definitely her alright, there was no mistaking that long red coat she always wore and from where he stood, he could even smell that particular brand of perfume, what was it? Ah yes, that's right, Zambra, he'd even tried to find it in the shops for some strange reason. He thought to himself, question after question in his head.

Was this really the moment he'd waited for all those weeks or should he try again next week. What if it all went wrong, what if she hadn't been in town tonight, what if it wasn't her? It had to be her of course, he knew her every move, he'd tracked her down before. Could he possibly wait another week? A voice inside his head reminded him that this was the moment he'd waited for and not to be such a fool.

He'd gone over and over the entire sequence of events in his mind. It had to be now, why wait any longer she'd humiliated him enough times in the past and now it was his turn, his turn to do the laughing, his turn to wipe that grin off her smirking face, his turn to get his revenge for turning him down in the first place and making him look a fool in front of everyone.

In his mind this was his night.

Part 1

Chapter 1

Buckley, North Wales, Two Weeks Earlier
Saturday, 11th November 1967 5.15pm

Have you seen my new shoes Mum? I've looked everywhere and I can't find them anywhere. I'm going to miss the damn bus if I don't get a move on. Sid and Jonno will be waiting for me and they'll probably go on ahead without me,' came the shout from the top of the stairs.

'No, I haven't seen your damn shoes Alan,' came the brusque reply from the front room, 'they are probably where you blooming well left them. I mean how old are you? Eighteen years of age! I could understand it if you were five. In fact, you were less trouble when you were five. Anyway, why do you need a bus to go to the Tivoli yer lazy sod, it's only up the road? Now shush be quiet for once, I'm trying to watch the start of this new Doctor Who episode, it's just started.'

'I told you before Mum, we are not going to the Tiv tonight, it's Chester for a change. Anyway, I've found them now, they were under the bed,' came the muffled response from the bedroom.

Alan slipped on the smart new pair of black Cuban heels he'd recently bought and gave them a quick polish with what had been his clean handkerchief. They fitted like a glove, bit tight at first but they certainly looked the business.

He went over to the bathroom cabinet and splashed some Brut aftershave on. As he stood in front of the wall mirror, checking himself over, he thought. *Oh yes, the new hipsters and the white button-down Ben Sherman shirt worked well together. I'm definitely in with a chance tonight particularly when I get in that ultra-violet glow of the disco lights.*

Alan Evans made his way down the stairs and into the small front room where his mother was sitting chomping her way through a small tray of broken toffee. She was completely engrossed in watching the old black and white TV which had certainly seen better days in the corner of the room.

'Toffee will do you no good Mum. Remember you nearly broke your dentures on those a few months ago, just go easy on it.'

'Are you still here? I was hoping for a nice peaceful Saturday night, there's no peace in this house.'

'Sorry I'm off now Mum, can you please tell Dad when you see him that I promise to pay him back for that loan next pay day,' replied Alan as he combed his hair and took one final look in the mirror on the welsh dresser.'

'Will do, hmm nice shoes our Alan better than those stupid winkle pickers you used to wear. God knows what they must have done to your feet and I dread to think how much you must have paid for them.'

'And a lot more comfortable Mum, I got a bargain according to Sid who said he'd…'

'Right, now shush be quiet, it's coming to an interesting bit here.'

'No, wait don't tell me, eh hang on are you sure you are not watching a "Carry on" film, that's Bernard Bresslaw isn't it?'

'Yes, it is actually, he does act in other things you know. I can't watch anything in peace. Now out you go me lad and don't be late. Don't you forget to catch the last bus home and please come in quietly as your dad will be home from a double shift at the steelworks and he'll be in bed. Oh, and another thing go easy on the drink we don't want a repeat of last weekend now do we?'

'Yes Mum, right Mum, three bags full Mum,' he muttered to himself as he grabbed his black leather jacket off the banister and made his way out of the house.

As soon as he left the house the cold wind hit him full on, he zipped his jacket up and thought to himself that winter was definitely now on its way.

He quickly headed down Bistre Avenue normally tree lined but now looking bare without the leaves that had long gone. As he crossed the road towards the town centre bus stop, he looked again at his watch and realised he really had to get a move on if he was to catch the next bus. It was cold, very cold in fact for the time of year and although it was only just after five thirty the night had already started to close in fast. The clocks had been put back an hour a couple of weeks back heralding the real arrival of autumn and winter.

As he got nearer to the bus stop, he could see his old school mates Sid and Jonno who were seated on the old wooden bench in front of the library waiting for him. They were chattering away like two old men. The three of them had been lifelong friends attending primary, secondary and even Sunday school together.

'What time do you call this Evo?' shouted Sid,' we've just missed one of the buses having to wait for you. Any later and we were about to give up on the Chester trip and head to the Tiv instead without you. We were just chatting about whether we had time to go and grab a quick beer across the road in the Black Lion.'

'Yeah, I'm sorry about this,' replied Evo,' I dozed off this afternoon in front of the fire and if it hadn't been for my mum waking me, I'd have probably still been there. Oh, happy birthday Jonno by the way, I had almost forgot, it's legal for you now then?'

'It is indeed. Cheers mate, anyway what's that smell Evo?' asked Jonno laughing and sniffing the air and wafting his hand, knowing full well where the after-shave smell was coming from.

'What smell? I don't know what you are on about! It's just a little something I dabbed on for the ladies this evening, works like a babe magnet apparently, well according to the adverts although not that I need it of course,' smirked Evo with an air of confidence.

'I don't think you are really meant to splash it all over. I'm surprised you can even breathe with that lot on. Well, let's hope it works for all of us, there seems to be enough of it to go around,' laughed Jonno out loud, 'I tell you what though to be honest I wouldn't mind a night at the Tivoli tonight instead, at least we can walk home from there. Come on what do you think?'

'Sod off Jonno, we go there most weeks, you'll have to give old Mickey the DJ a miss tonight, it won't do you any harm. We promised ourselves a night in Chester this week and that's what we are doing. In any case the bus will be here in a minute.'

'I can't understand why we are not even going by car, it'd be quicker. I mean what's the point in you spending all that money on lessons and then passing your test Sid? You said we'd have complete freedom once you passed your test, a chance to see the world you said! I thought we'd be going further afield by now like Rhyl or Talacre or somewhere?'

'Look it might be quicker Jonno but haven't you been reading the papers lately? I'm afraid those days have gone with the introduction of that breathalyser thing the other week. Yer can't take any chances these days mate I can tell you. The rozzers will be after me like a shot and I for one am not going to risk it. I wouldn't be able to have a beer or two with you pair. I'd have to sit there and watch you lot enjoying yourselves. Anyway, Rhyl will be cold this time of year, it is November you know.'

'I wasn't thinking about sitting on the bloody beach mate, there are a few nightclubs and discos there that are still open you know even in the winter,' replied Jonno as he kicked an imaginary football against the library wall.

'I'm not sure his beaten up old thing would have got us there anyway,' snorted Evo sarcastically

'Course it would, it's a great little motor, just needs a little bit of TLC that's all.'

'And a new engine of course Sid!'

'Just look at the time anyway we should have been in the pub now downing our first pint,' chipped in Jonno changing the subject and pointing up to the clock above the old library steps.

'Come on, never mind all that, here comes the bus,' said Sid. 'Do you know I can already taste that first pint, it probably won't even touch the sides. Come on chaps, last one on is a cissy. Just a pity Glyn couldn't have joined us, man flu apparently or something like that.'

'Yeah shame that, he'd have enjoyed an evening in Chester,' said Evo holding out his arm for the bus driver to stop who had every intention of stopping for them anyway.

The three of them climbed aboard the Crosville double decker bus and just managed to find a seat right at the back upstairs. The bus was noisy and packed out with the usual partygoers heading to the city centre for a Saturday night out.

There was a strong smell of fish and chips as one or two of the passengers had decided to have an early tea or a late lunch on the way. It was so busy upstairs the conductor had a job making his way through the crowd to collect the fares.

Soon they were heading past the Hawker Siddeley aircraft factory at Broughton and heading down the long straight road in the direction of Saltney. On the right-hand side, they could now see and smell the huge bonfires that were blazing away in the fields.

'It bloody well stinks around here and I don't mean your aftershave this time Evo,' sniffed Jonno getting up to close the small side window.

'Well, what do you expect Jonno? If you want my opinion, they…' remarked Sid.

'We don't!' came back the reply in unison.

'Come on, I mean it's a damn shame this foot and mouth epidemic can't be sorted out in some other way like vaccination or something,' continued Sid, 'I mean it must be heart breaking for these farmers having to destroy their cattle.

It's their livelihood after all and I shouldn't wonder if some of them never get over it.'

'The government will help them out with funding surely?' responded Evo, 'I mean they won't be out of pocket, will they?'

'That's not the point, they'll have to start all over again and some of them will think it's not even worth it. It will take years before the farming industry gets over this, you'll see. I'm just glad I didn't go into farming after leaving school.'

'It started in Shropshire, in, er, Oswestry apparently last month. Well, that's what I read in the paper anyway,' replied Jonno, 'but amazing how the damn disease has spread so fast across the country. The smell is dreadful, I think I'm going to be sick.'

'Keep it for later mate, a pint will soon sort you out, we'll be there soon.'

Twenty minutes later and having stopped at almost every bus stop en-route the packed bus finally pulled into Bridge Street, Chester where there was already a queue of weary hardworking shop assistants and shoppers waiting to make the return journey home.

Everyone piled off the bus in a somewhat disorderly manner all heading off in their various directions and eager to get that first drink in.

'So where to first?' asked Jonno, 'Well, I quite fancy the Dublin Packet or maybe the Clockwork Orange for starters, we haven't been in either of those for a while. Do you know I have a strange feeling that I might just tap on tonight!'

'Well, you are not likely to in the Dublin Packet mate. It has to be the Boathouse of course, we'll have a swift one in there and then make our way up through the park to

Quaintways later on!' replied Sid who was already heading down Lower Bridge Street towards the river bank.

'Hang on Sid, can't we just go to a pub nearer the city centre. It's out of our way down there, we're walking for the sake of it!' shouted Evo who was reluctantly following behind by about three yards and wanted to stay at least a bit nearer the city centre pubs and clubs.

'No, come on Evo, we'll be there in a minute and the walk will do you good, you look as though you could do with some exercise, you are starting to get a bit of a beer belly on you!'

'Cheeky sod, I get enough exercise in the week humping stuff in work mate!'

It was relatively quiet as they walked alongside the River Dee with just a few of the local leisure boat owners securing their crafts and locking them up for the evening. With the onset of winter, the boat owners had to work longer hours and pick up any passing trade they could but they always managed to keep themselves busy.

The summer however was a very different kettle of fish altogether with large crowds of tourists all enjoying the fine weather down at the river front and long queues waiting to board the pleasure going vessels. Ten minutes later the trio arrived at the Boathouse pub and managed to push their way through the crowd to finally get to the bar. It was busy as expected with some hardy souls taking their drinks to the outside area.

They stood for a while and waited to be served at the bar, eventually managing to find a vacant table inside overlooking the river.

'I tell you what boys, I don't know about you but I feel out of place here. We should have gone into one of the pubs in the city centre or just stayed in Buckley,' said Evo, 'the birds in here seem a bit snobby, stuck up for my liking.'

'Don't be ridiculous Evo, it's just your imagination. Look, just relax and enjoy the view.' said Sid who was now eyeing up a dark-haired girl in a very short tartan mini-skirt and tight white blouse that he'd spotted sitting on the next table.

He had tried a few times to catch her eye but she just wasn't interested and in fact was trying her best to ignore him.

***

Chester City Centre

Detective Chief Inspector Michael Sheraton was off duty and enjoying a quiet meal in the city centre with his wife Jane in a cosy restaurant known as the Grotto. A delightful little restaurant tucked away up on the rows in Bridge Street.

The restaurant was quieter than usual although it was still early evening and it was soon likely to be fully booked. This was one place in the city however where Michael always felt relaxed away from the hustle and bustle. It was also a place where he was very unlikely to bump into any of his punters past and present.

'It's always relaxing in here Mike, good food, lovely music, not too intrusive and away from the busy pubs.'

'You're right and just think in three months' time love, I will have finally retired and we can start planning those foreign holidays that we've talked so much about,' said Michael softly not looking up as he pored over the menu as he wondered whether to go for the steak or the chicken.

'Well, I've got some news for you darling,' replied Jane excitedly, 'Guess what, I've already been down to the travel agents and picked up the latest Clarkson overseas brochures. I've even shortlisted the Spanish resorts we should be thinking about. Sun, Sea and Sex in that order, sounds great doesn't it?'

'Okay, maybe not the sex,' laughed Jane as she picked up her wine glass and chinked it against his in a silent toast.

'Eh keep your voice down love and hang on a minute, you're a bit of a fast worker Mrs Sheraton! I haven't even resigned from the force yet or for that matter even told old Duckworth I'm even thinking of finishing. He will probably want me to stay on you know, they will need to think about recruiting my replacement.'

'Yes, I know that love but these things have to be booked in advance you know, Lloret Del Mar is starting to become very popular and much in demand these days. I mean we don't want to be last minute, do we? It'll be a nice start to your retirement, two weeks on the Costa Brava. You know you owe it to yourself Michael, you deserve a decent break with the hours that you have put in recently. Anyway, my glass is almost empty, another glass of Mateus Rose please darling, you are slacking a bit as a wine waiter.'

'Well, I suppose you are right love,' he replied as he topped up both glasses, 'we should plan it now and after all you only retire once in your life, I think! Although do you know I wouldn't mind doing something a bit different but maybe related, after all it's a long time before the old state pension kicks in you know.'

'You need some high-quality relaxation time first love. Anyway, you can tell Assistant Chief Constable Duckworth of your plans when you get back into the office next week. Now in the meantime make your mind up quick, the waitress is hovering over there waiting for us to order.'

***

Steve Robbins and Gordon Jones took their usual places at the smart entrance to the plush nightclub in the city in readiness for the nine o'clock rush. Steve who was always well dressed, worked in the day as an aircraft fitter at the Hawker Siddeley factory at Broughton but at weekends he worked as a bouncer or as he laughingly preferred to call it a *Security Access Executive*.

Gordon on the other hand was out of full-time work and no matter how hard he tried he always looked like a sack of potatoes or as though he had just got out of bed which probably wasn't far from the truth. If there was any nonsense at the door Steve had been trained to use his well-rehearsed communication and conflict resolution skills before, or rather than, resorting to brute force. Gordon, however was no stranger to a fight and tended to sort an incident out using his fists, his broken nose carrying the evidence.

The combination of the two men however worked well together with Steve handling it first diplomatically and if all else fails, Gordon would then step in as a finale act. The doors on this particular evening were not due to open until 8.45 and a queue had already started to form on the pavement outside. It was now starting to spill out across the road. Gordon looked at his watch, it was just after 8.35.

'What do you think Steve, shall we let them in early? They are getting a bit noisy and impatient out here. It can't do any harm can it? They are a bit lively for my liking. At least it will get them off the street and out of our way.'

'No fear mate, we are under strict instructions not to open those doors just yet. Anyway, the bands will still be doing their final sound checks at the moment. The boss would have our guts for garters if we open the doors now. Calm down Gordon, it's still far too early yet. Relax mate, it's a Saturday night they are all just out enjoying themselves.'

'Aye, I suppose your right.'

'You seem a bit depressed tonight Gordon, what's bothering you, it's not love troubles again?'

'No, nothing like that, I still haven't got over how Chester lost away to York City this afternoon 4 – 1, I mean four bleeding one against York City. I hope that's not a sign of things to come.'

'Let's hope not. Probably just a bad day at the office.'

The two men stood there guarding the main entrance, they were too busy talking about the day's other football results to see someone sneaking into the club down a side entrance.

***

Two hours later.

Jonno and Evo had just finished their last round of drinks and had already started making their way through the crowd and out of the Boathouse pub. They had got fed up waiting for Sid who was determined to have a good night out and in fact was still at the bar rushing down what was now his fourth pint of Wrexham Lager. He downed the last pint as if he was in some sort of a race, belched as quietly as he could and hastily tried to catch the others up. He legged it out of the pub and caught them just outside the park gates.

They were hoping to take a short cut through the nearby Grosvenor Park but it was now closed for the winter so they had to resort to a quick detour. The huge wrought iron gates at the entrance were now firmly chained and padlocked until the following morning as part of the park's new winter opening or to be more exact their early winter closing programme.

They headed instead around the perimeter of the well-kept park, even in autumn it was well tended and cared for by the park gardeners. They walked in the direction of Love Street and then turned left onto the busy Foregate Street. As they continued onwards under the Eastgate Street Clock they were tempted to visit some of the other hostelries on the way but time simply didn't permit and, in any case, Jonno somehow had got it into his head that it was to be his lucky night on the dance floor.

Just five minutes later they arrived in Northgate Street just outside Quaintways where a long queue had already begun to form outside on the pavement. The nightclub was always a popular venue particularly on a Saturday night with young people coming from far and near with two floors of live music and a buffet on the ground floor. It was a great place to spend an evening out. At times it was as if Cheshire, North Wales and even further afield descended on the city.

'Okay chaps,' said Jonno as he rummaged through his pockets, 'I've been looking forward to this all week. Now look before we get in there which floor do you fancy tonight when we do eventually get in? Assuming we will get in of course, as soon as this damn queue shifts.'

'Keep your voice down Jonno, else the bouncers will be turfing you out before you've even got your foot in the door,' whispered Sid.

'They don't scare me, well not much anyway.' laughed Jonno as he lit up another Players No.6 cigarette and tossed the match into the road.

'Well, where do you reckon the talent will be?' shouted Evo above the chattering excitement as they now took their place in the queue.

'Well, it'll be packed as usual but I fancy listening to a local band on the top floor tonight. I can't remember their name but I think they are from Wrexham. I saw them here a few weeks back with the Wall City Jazzmen,' replied Sid who was now leaning against a wall and looking somewhat the worse for wear as he also casually lit up another fag.

'I didn't mean that sort of talent, dumbo,' replied Evo as the queue edged slowly forward before coming to an abrupt halt.

'I know what you mean,' laughed Sid eyeing up an attractive short haired blonde that he'd just caught sight of at the head of the queue.

'Top floor it is then and we'll take it from there. Aye up lads we're on the move at last, they have just opened the doors.'

The queue moved rapidly forward and Quaintways in the city centre was now buzzing. By day it was a delightful restaurant/café serving afternoon tea to weary shoppers but by night it became a superb live music venue. It regularly played host to the huge acts of the day Status Quo, Kenny Ball,

Fleetwood Mac to name just a few. Tonight was also a special night with Jonno celebrating his 18th birthday but in a different sort of way.

The queue for the entrance soon went down and the three mates were finally inside the nightclub and queuing this time instead at the bar. Jonno who was a stocky six-footer squeezed his way through to the front and within seconds waving a pound note in his hand managed to catch the eye of one of the bar staff.

'My round boys, three pints of Carling please luv,' said Jonno to the barmaid.

'No, hang on, wait a minute, get me a large whisky on the rocks instead Jonno. I just feel a bit bloated with all that lager. Hang on where's she gone, I saw her over there a minute or two ago?' said Sid not taking a breath and who was still frantically searching across the dance floor for the girl that he'd first spotted in the queue outside.

'Whisky! C'mon it's a bit early Sid for a double whisky but alright being as it's my birthday.'

'Just the two pints then and a double whisky on the rocks please love,' said Jonno to the barmaid as she waited patiently for confirmation of the order.

'Actually, you do know it should be you buying me a drink Sid, it is my birthday after all! Anyway, that girl you were eyeing up has probably gone up to the top floor by now.'

Sid and Evo wandered over to a table on the other side of the function room.

Jonno paid for the drinks with the one-pound note, collected his change and carefully manoeuvred his way back through the crowd carefully holding the two-pint glasses and the large whisky between his hands.

'Bit pricey in here Evo, a pint is just over two shillings here and it's only a shilling and ten pence down the road. And as for your whisky, Sid...'

But Sid was now totally engrossed with the blonde girl he'd seen in the queue, in fact he'd had a good look round and saw her in the far corner. He'd eventually spotted her dancing with one of her girlfriends.

After downing the large whisky in one go, he plucked up courage and strolled over in her direction, well almost tripped over to her on the dancefloor. She had no interest in him whatsoever, pretended to ignore him and continued to dance with her girlfriend.

As he approached her on the dance floor, he decided to try out one of his many unrehearsed chat up lines that he'd been working on.

'I don't suppose I could have the last dance with you?'

'Yeah, of course, well actually you're having it,' came the quick-witted response.

Smart arse, he thought but decided not to be put off with her comments and to go along with her in any case. He'd seen it in the movies how a bad introduction can eventually blossom into a most wonderful relationship. The girlfriend that she had been dancing with had taken the hint, picked up her handbag and by now had quietly slinked off back to the bar leaving them alone to chat on the dance floor.

'I haven't sheen you in here before, do you come here often?' said Sid doing his very best to avoid slurring his words.

'It's my first time here. I've just moved into the area,' replied the girl as she continued to show absolutely no interest in him and stared down at the dancefloor.

'Oh, you'll enjoy this place, it's got great live music with Jazz night on Mondays,' said Sid who was now having difficult in even stringing his words together never mind standing up to dance.

Meanwhile he hadn't noticed Evo and Jonno were now sat at a table watching his every move and laughing at him from a distance.

Sid was now well and truly stuck for words, well meaningful ones anyway. He was thinking of how next to continue this conversation but before he had even chance to say anything...

'Yes, I'll definitely come here again. I must tell my boyfriend about this place, he'd love it.' she said as she continuously chewed her gum and writhed to the sound of Diana Ross and the Supremes.

Sid looked gutted and just then something inside him snapped. He thought to himself, *Enough is enough, there's no point in wasting anymore time here. There are other fish in the sea.* He muttered something like '*you were a crap dancer anyway*' and without any warning staggered back over to the bar leaving the girl dancing on her own. Norman Wisdom would have been proud of his impersonation.

'Give me another double whisky on the rocks,' he snapped at the barmaid who was busy serving another customer.

'What's the magic word?' replied the barmaid who was actually considering whether she should even serve him in the state he was in. He could hardly stand up now and was holding tight with both hands onto the polished brass bar handrail.

'Abrabloodycadabra, now come on wench and get me a drink fast. I'm parched. I could die of thirst in this damn place!' shouted Sid impatiently as he banged the top of the bar.

'Okay sunshine out you go now, you've had quite enough to drink,' replied the barmaid who wasn't prepared to put up with being spoken to in that manner, 'Come on, out you go before I have to call security to throw you out.'

'Don't bother love and you can shove your drink up yer arse,' belched Sid who was already at the top of the stairs by this point and clinging onto a hand rail for dear life.

Jonno and Evo looked on in sheer amazement, they had never seen Sid in that sort of state before.

'Come on, we really should go after him,' said Jonno, 'we can't leave him like this.'

'Clear off Jonno, he's the one who has stamped off and left us! We'll probably see him at the bus stop later on or knowing him he'll probably get the last train back. Come on, I'm just starting to enjoy myself. Anyway, by the look of the state of him the fresh air will do him good, sober him up a bit I'd have thought. Come on, it's my round sup up, at least it's now a cheaper one.' replied Evo who had no intention whatsoever of chasing after him.'

***

Rowton Church
Sunday, 12th November 1967

The Sheraton family, Mike, Jane and their daughter Janet were all regular attendees at the local church and they were up bright and early in readiness for the morning service. Sunday mornings were always that bit special in the Sheraton household and followed a strict regime – a lie in until 8.30, a full English breakfast and then the three of them all dressed smartly heading off to church which was a short drive away. In the summer they would walk the short distance but this time of year they nearly always elected to drive.

Later they would pick up the Sunday papers on their way back for a relaxing afternoon in front of the log fire. Up until a few years ago Michael had always said he didn't haven't much time for the clergy but he had had a complete change of mind after the way the church and the congregation had supported and looked after his dear old mother following his father's death. His mother, now a regular churchgoer normally accompanied them until recently before she moved into retirement apartments in Colwyn Bay. The Reverend Ian Edwards was there as usual to greet the congregation as they came through the arched doorway.

'Good morning and how is your mother Michael, I assume she has settled in her new place up on the North Wales coast?'

'Yes, very well, thanks Reverend, yes, she has settled in nicely, she has always enjoyed that part of North Wales and we always knew she wanted to move there. She has a lot of friends over there and will be attending church this morning over in Old Colwyn I shouldn't wonder. I'll tell her you were asking after her,' replied Michael Sheraton as he shook hands and was about to make his way into the church.

'Yes, you tell her it will be good to see her again. She is in our thoughts and prayers. We often talk about her, a lovely lady. Perhaps when the weather improves, she might make the trip back here and attend the morning service with us, it would be really good to see her?'

'I think it's just a little bit too far for her to make the weekly trip to be honest and I think her old car would have trouble getting up that steep Rhuallt hill, but I'm sure she'll be coming over for a weekend with us. When she does, I'm sure she'll be coming back to the church. She has lovely memories of this place and the support you kindly gave her,' smiled Michael as he collected the hymn books from the shelf at the back.

'Still I hear you'll be retiring soon so perhaps we might see her when she comes over to stop with you?'

'Erm, yes, that's right but not just yet,' said Michael turning around sharply as they made their way to their regular pew down towards the front of the church.

'How on earth does he know about my pending retirement Jane?' he whispered, 'I'm trying to keep the lid on that. I'm trying to keep it all quiet at the moment. No one is supposed to know that.'

'Well, perhaps I might have just mentioned it in passing Mike.'

'Perhaps! Well, let's keep this quiet for now, even the force don't know yet.'

Chapter 2

Shotton, North Wales
Monday, 13th November 1967, 5.40am

The old double decker bus creaked up the short incline and pulled into the steelworks bus terminus just outside the wages department at the top yard. It was where all the local buses from miles around converged at the start of a new shift. It was a few minutes behind schedule, something to do with an oil pressure light coming on just before they left Buckley, but nevertheless was just in time for everyone to catch their ongoing internal bus transfers to their various departments.

The John Summers steelworks which only months ago had been nationalised as part of the British Steel Corporation was huge with all the departments spread over several miles across the site. Now employing over 12,000 men it was one of the largest employers in the area. The articulated internal buses were all lined up in readiness and packed as usual but at that time of day, the conversation on the buses of the early morning 6-till-2 shift was virtually nil; in fact, most of the shift workers were still waking up before their eight-hour shift began.

Evo and Jonno made their way to the furnace stage bus.

'See you later on Sid, we might catch you for a beer after work in the Black Lion, usual time if you fancy one?' shouted Evo as he was about to step aboard the internal works bus.

Sid grumbled something to them, nodded and made his way across the yard to clock on at the top yard time office passing close by to the General Engineering building.

Jonno and Evo took their seats on the hard wooden benches which ran down the centre of the bus. As they sat waiting to depart an old man at their side decided he couldn't wait for breakfast any longer and munched his way through a cheese and onion sandwich. Through the window they could still see men making a last-minute dash to the bus terminal across the iron bridge which spanned the river Dee.

'I must say Jonno, Sid didn't have much to say for himself and to be honest he looked a bit worse for wear this morning. It looks to me as though he didn't get much sleep last night. I mean at least he did have yesterday to get over Saturday's hangover.'

'Yeah, you're right he didn't have much to say, it's not like him. I asked him about Saturday night, he said he hadn't got a clue how he got home. All he remembers was waking up on the settee yesterday afternoon. You do know he's having trouble with his step mum at home, don't you?'

'No, I hadn't realised that, he's never mentioned that before.'

'Yeah, he does keep a lot of it bottled up to be honest. Apparently, he's never seen eye to eye with her and I think it probably won't be too long before he gets thrown out of the house the way things are going there. He only uses it as a place to sleep anyway, he never eats at home if he can help it, his mum never makes him anything.'

'Really, I hadn't realised that. He's certainly been acting odd of late, you're right it's not like him at all. Anyway, I enjoyed Saturday night it was good although I can't remember much about it to be honest. I must have had a right skin full, I had a terrible hangover yesterday and had spent most of it in bed!'

'You're right, it was a great night wasn't it. We must do it again mate.'

Some ten minutes later the articulated bus arrived at the open-hearth furnaces but there was no big rush to get off. The men stepped off the bus and made their way one by one in an orderly procession across to the time office, they each picked out their individual clock cards and clocked on for their early morning shift. As they made their way up onto the furnace stage itself the heat of the furnaces hit them full on. Some of the night shift had already started making their way down towards the waiting buses. The new shift personnel had only been on the furnace stage for a few minutes and already their clothing sparkled with the particles of fine metal dust which hung in the air. The new shift made their way down into the locker room next to the small canteen area.

'Do you fancy a brew before we get started lads, I'm blooming parched meself?' uttered old Reg the chargehand who was already filling up the kettle and who was always keen to have breakfast first, 'get that bacon out of my knapsack Jonno, there's enough for the three of us and make sure you get it onto the clean shovel this time, I had bits in me mouth after the last time you did it. I'm sure we could all murder a bacon butty. You'll find a sliced loaf in me bag.'

'Will do Reg, I must admit I could eat a horse between two bread vans.' laughed Jonno as he stepped back onto the furnace stage area.

He grabbed hold of the nearest clean shovel, gave it a quick wipe with his sleeve just in case and placed the bacon slices accordingly. He then briefly opened the furnace door. The heat was immense and within minutes probably more like seconds the bacon was done and breakfast was ready for serving.

The men still bleary eyed sat there in the canteen drinking their mugs of hot tea and munching in silence but the meal was short-lived.

'Okay you lot out you go there is work to be done. You've only just arrived on shift, you should have had your breakfast before you got here. You'll have time for a break later on,' bellowed the foreman as he burst in through the door.

***

Buckley Cross
Monday, 13th November 1967, 5.15pm

Jonno pushed open the door of The Black Lion inn. The bar was pretty much empty apart from a couple of lads quietly playing darts in the corner. This was no real surprise as a Monday evening was always a quiet night for trade for most of the pubs in the town. Even the jukebox was silent. The Black Lion however was a popular pub well situated in the town centre and at this time of day it was normally frequented by those who were either on their days off or just having a beer or two relaxing after working the morning shift. Jonno ordered himself a pint of bitter and while he was waiting for it to be poured, strolled over to the wall mounted jukebox.

He selected *"Baby, now that I've found you by the Foundations"* and collected his pint off the bar. He took his drink over to a table in the far corner by the window, lit up a cigarette and started leafing through the morning daily newspaper which presumably had been left there by a previous customer.

The newspaper seemed to be full of stories of the Foot and Mouth disease with new farms in the area being affected each day. Soldiers had now been drafted into a number of areas to spread disinfectant across farm yards and entrances. The disease was now spreading rapidly like wildfire. All markets were now shut and no one was being allowed onto farms. The government had insisted on closing footpaths, halting country sports, angling, shooting and hunting. Even road construction programmes were being halted to free up vehicles and machinery to dispose of the slaughtered stock.

Jonno shook his head as he leafed through page after page of bad news his thoughts were with the farmers and the workers who were struggling to overcome the situation. Just then the door opened and it was Evo looking a bit bleary eyed as if he'd just got out of bed. Jonno glanced at his watch as if to say what time do you call this.

'Didn't you get me one in then Jonno?' said Evo examining the table for his pint.

'No sorry Evo I wasn't sure when you were arriving. Here get whatever you want and stop your bloody moaning,' replied Jonno as he pushed a ten-shilling note across the table.

'Cheers mate, I'm gasping I can tell you.'

Immediately after getting served Evo took a large mouthful of lager at the bar and came and sat down next to Jonno.

They both sat there in silence for a moment.

'So, don't I get any change then Evo?'

'Oh yeah sorry mate, I had completely forgot. To tell you the truth I'm still a bit sleepy eyed at the moment. I only managed to get about an hour's kip this afternoon when I got home. Some sod next door was drilling and banging. I tell you there is no consideration for shift workers. I'll see if he likes it when I come home late at night,' replied Evo as he handed over the change. 'Eh, I don't suppose you've heard from Sid at all?'

'No nothing mate, I saw him on the bus coming back home momentarily. He didn't have much to say for himself. I reminded him we were having a beer in here early doors and I'm a bit surprised he's not in here before me to be quite honest.'

'Yeah, strange he doesn't seem to be speaking to me at the moment, I haven't a clue what I've done wrong. Still that's his loss. He's probably avoiding us and gone down to the Lane End working men's club.'

'Ah leave him, he would have been here by now. He gets moods like that you know. I remember he used to get them in school you know, give him a couple of days and he'll soon be back to normal you watch. It can't be girlfriend trouble as he hasn't got one at present.'

'Perhaps that's his problem, anyway sup up it's my round.' replied Evo, 'I've got quite a thirst on I can tell you, that one didn't even touch the sides!'

'Same again ta mate. Eh, how do you fancy going back to Chester next weekend perhaps try a different pub or club this time?'

'No thanks mate, whilst I enjoyed it, it was good to get out of town for once in a while but I tell you this it will be good to be back to the old Tiv this weekend and we can walk home from there instead of rushing for that last bus. That's what I fancy anyway, all being well of course.

***

Tivoli night club, Buckley
Saturday, 18th November 1967

'You can't come in here dressed like that,' bellowed the bouncer on the door, 'we do have a dress code in this place you know!'

Evo looked down at himself and looked quite puzzled, he thought about replying back with '*pity you lot are not following it then*' but realised that the door would be as far as he would get if he took that approach. Underneath his full-length ex air force coat, he was wearing an orange grandad vest and heavily flared denim jeans. The jeans which had been modified somewhat with a floral material insert providing something like thirty-inch bottoms. 'What's wrong with these, my mum sewed them in for me especially. They are all the rage.'

'Ruined a good pair of jeans if you ask me and to be honest, they would make a nice pair of curtains for someone would be my best guess. What's the material anyway? Been to a jumble sale or is it one of your mum's old frocks.'

The two bouncers stood there laughing and pointing at Evo whilst waving other party goers into the club.

Evo stood there like a spare part waiting for the go ahead he knew that if he stood there long enough, he would get in eventually.

'Look I'll let it go this time. It's dark in there hopefully so no one will notice, try and stand in a dark corner.' They all stood in silence for a minute. 'Oh go on then. It's your lucky night. Go on, in you go, try and stand in a dark corner! Behave yourself and I'll pretend I haven't seen you!'

Evo silently mouthed the word '*Tosser*' and joined Jonno who was now patiently waiting for him inside the nightclub.

'I think they look great, he's got no taste and needs to get some modern fashion sense, he needs a pair of lucky jeans,' said Evo as he stood admiring himself up and down.

'Do you know, he did have a point, they do stand out a bit and by the looks of it there is only you wearing anything like them,' replied Jonno as they gradually inched their way towards the front of the bar.

'There's no sign of Sid, I don't suppose?' said Evo looking around and wishing to change the subject.

'No, haven't seen him, he could have made his own way here I suppose.'

They had just managed to get served and carried their pints of Carling lager through to the dance floor which was now heaving. A local rock group from Sandycroft was blasting through their own rendition of *Green Tambourine* and had only been on stage for about ten minutes when a group of youths quite close to Evo and Jonno had been dancing amongst themselves, then suddenly started arguing with each other. Voices were raised but couldn't be heard above the volume of the amplifiers but all of a sudden, all hell broke loose and within seconds the security staff arrived to remove the offenders.

The band took a quick impromptu break and left the stage. DJ Mickey had a bird's eye view of the action from his perch high above the dance floor and was about to step in by playing a record or two but within minutes following evictions all was back to normal and the band were soon back on stage continuing as if nothing had happened.

'Phew, that was close,' said Evo, 'a few seconds earlier and we'd have been in the middle of that lot!'

'Must be your lucky jeans mate!'

Chapter 3

Saltney, Nr Chester, Two Weeks Later
Saturday, 25th November 1967, 5.30pm

Jennifer Webb was rushing to finish work as a shop assistant at the local co-op grocery store and she was now running very late. She certainly had to get a move on if she had any chance of getting into the city centre on time to do her evening job. Just as she had been about to leave the shop for home, they had received an unexpected delivery from the wholesalers and she had been faced with no choice but to help her boss unload the fresh produce. Her boss Norman was not a bad old stick but he relied heavily on Jennifer who was always keen to help out if she could. Norman Arrowsmith was now in his fifties, a shy unconfirmed bachelor who actually fancied Jennifer like mad but knew he must be at the back of any queue. Norman had been badly crippled following a motorbike accident in his teens but despite this he always managed to get around the store albeit a bit slower than the rest of the staff.

'Well, if that's all Norman, I'll be off now. I'm really quite exhausted, it's been a busy old day today. I'll be glad of a rest and it's not even over for me yet. Oh, and I've tidied up the bacon counter for you and it's nice and clean ready for next week. Do you know, I could do with a nice break somewhere, somewhere warm with a nice beach. I hate this time of the year, a bit of sun on my back would be lovely and recharge the old batteries. Anyway, don't you work too hard Norman and you have a great weekend.'

Norman had a lot on his mind and was still busy doing a final count on the stock in the adjacent storeroom in readiness for the area management visit. 'Oh right, yes, goodnight Jennifer. Thanks for staying on love and helping me, you look like you could use a good holiday, you take good care of yourself,' he responded as he came back into the shop. He closed the till and tidied up the counter. He couldn't resist eyeing her up lustfully and watching her every step as she left the shop and closed the door. He limped over to the doorway, pulled down the blinds, reversed the OPEN sign, pulled across the heavy bolts and finally locked up for the weekend. He stood for a moment, paused and thought on how attractive she was.

Jennifer took a quick look at her watch, she had to dash home as quickly as she could. She had planned to call her old school friend Anne Barlow to have a good old chin wag before heading off to her evening shift but time didn't permit and in any case the telephone box at the end of the street was once again out of order through vandalism.

With just enough time to grab a quick bite to eat and get changed from her work clothes she eventually set off back to the bus stop, praying she hadn't missed the bus into the city centre.

She was in luck however as she turned the corner, she could see a few people still waiting at the bus stop. The bus had been delayed for some unknown reason and was now running some ten minutes later than usual. The early evening

Crosville bus was packed with standing room only but it didn't matter it was a short journey into the city centre. An elderly gentleman wearing a strange tweed trilby doffed his hat and kindly offered her his seat as she moved down the bus but Jennifer declined, she was happy to stand.

Fifteen minutes later it pulled into the bus stop in Lower Bridge Street and everyone piled off as if they were all late. She ran as fast as she could up Bridge Street up to the cross and turned into Northgate Street, she almost bounced up the steps to the half-timbered galleries known locally as the "rows" and arrived just in time for the start of her shift running the disco bar at the city centre nightclub.

Jennifer was a conscientious employee, a hard worker and was very reliable. She had worked at the club since leaving school and was well thought of by both of her employers. She was popular at the club, constantly chatted up at the bar and had no shortage of admirers but had no time for boyfriends any more, in fact very little time for socialising at all.

A few months earlier Jennifer and her jealous boyfriend Neil from her school days had broken up, she thought at the time it was the end of the world but she was over it all now. Life had moved on for her.

For now, Jennifer Webb had only one thing on her mind, she was saving hard with any spare money she had for a deposit on her own flat. The shabby cold one bedroomed flat she rented although convenient for the city centre was in a very sorry state with no central heating and was bitterly cold in the winter. She was always glad to get to work, at least that way she could keep warm.

***

Mill House Farm, Saughall Nr Chester

Mill House Farm had been in the Smith family for over three generations and nineteen-year-old Ken Smith had recently taken over the day to day running of the thirty-acre farm from his father Albert who was no longer able to manage it on his own. It was a huge responsibility on his shoulders for someone so young but Ken was giving it his all.

Ken was the only son of Albert and Doreen Smith and he was keen to follow in his father's footsteps. Doreen had passed away just last year after a long illness. Albert had nursed and cared for her during her illness and he had never got over her death but at least the farm helped to take his mind off it.

Farming was in Ken's blood; in fact, he'd not known anything else growing up on a busy working farm. He'd thought about going off to an agricultural college near Nantwich but his dad had persuaded him to stay and help on their own working farm. Even as a little boy he'd played with tractors, not toys but the real thing. There was never a thought when he left school about his career. Whether to work at the local Shotton steelworks or at the nearby Hawker Siddeley aircraft factory never entered his head. No, Kenneth David Smith was destined to help his father on the dairy farm and he was loving every minute of it until this dreadful Foot and Mouth disease had also hit the county.

They thought that they had somehow escaped the disease with only two of the surrounding farms reporting the problem a couple of weeks back. But it was only just a few days ago that Albert had noticed one of their cows seeming to struggle to eat its food while he was milking and he immediately called the vet. Sure enough, the checks revealed what Albert had feared and suspected – it was confirmed as Foot and Mouth disease. From that moment on their lives were in complete turmoil.

Ken had a work hard play hard philosophy, by day there was no harder worker but most weekends he would normally be off into Chester for a night drinking with his mates but there was no nightclubbing for Ken this weekend. Even the local young farmers club had temporarily suspended all of their social events with all farms now firmly in lock-down. All the farms had been run off their feet dealing with this appalling disease. It had been soul destroying, years of building up their farm businesses and then seeing their livestock being burnt in funeral pyres all around the country.

'We are really going to miss James tonight you know Kenneth, he's called in sick earlier on this morning and just when we really needed him.' Albert wasn't one for nicknames or short names and always called his son and anyone else for that matter by their full Christian name. 'Did you manage to bring in the extra farm hands that we need for tonight otherwise we are going to struggle with this lot on our own?' asked Albert who was now busy making himself a pot of tea in the kitchen and still hadn't quite come to terms with the huge task that lay ahead of them.

'I have Dad, don't worry about old Jim as the Nixon brothers have brought in one of their mates to help us out, we should be okay between us. I'm sure Jim will be back with us next week. It's not like him you know,' replied Ken shaking his head, 'he has never missed a day in his life. With a bit of luck, we should be able to get the first stage at least finished by midnight all being well. I've also ordered the extra excavators for tomorrow. They should be with us first thing.'

'Well done Kenneth, I don't know what I'd do without you and those good, strong workers the Nixon boys. I'll say this they are just what we need for this lot. I remember their dad George, now he was a worker, strong as an ox he was, built like a brick whatsonames. Anyway, I was hoping by now we'd have seen an end to this epidemic and we could get on with farming as normal but it's going to be a while before that happens. Your old grandad would be turning in his grave if he'd seen what we are now having to go through with this lot. It's a damn shame, a bloody shame that's what it is.'

'Cheer up, we can start again Dad, it'll take time but you mark my words we'll soon have this farm back to how it was, trust me, you'll be proud of what we can all achieve when we really put our minds to it. This time next year we will be back to normal, you'll see.'

'I'm glad to hear someone is thinking positive. Do you know Kenneth, I must admit if I didn't have you to take over the farm, I'd be thinking of selling up and retiring now. I wouldn't be able to manage all this on my own,' tutted Albert as he stirred his large mug of tea. 'In any case you watch they'll be wanting to put houses on this ere land of ours soon, you see if I'm wrong son. There will be land agents for miles around crying out for a piece of this lot. I can see a day when people drive past here and say do you remember when there used to be cows in that field. There's nothing but all houses there now.'

Albert paused for a moment, shook his head, tutted to himself again and took a large sup of tea from his heavily stained mug.

'Any road as you say with a bit of luck old James Adams will be back at work next week.'

Albert had always referred to Jim Adams as old even though he was younger than himself.

'I'll tell you this though, he's picked a right time to go off ill. As you say in all the years, I've known him I don't ever remember him ever having a single day off sick and we do need that extra pair of hands with this lot I can tell you.'

'Now look, stop worrying Dad, Jim will be soon back at work and we'll be fine. The sooner we finish with this lot the better and if I have anything to do with it this land will remain as farm land in the Smith family for generations to come. Come on now Dad, are you really sure you want to get involved in this, you can stay in the house if you want you know? We can manage without you, you know. I will need to get over to the barn as the vet and the lads will be here anytime and we can't keep them waiting.'

'Yes, I'm sure I'll be okay son, I can't leave all this to you on your own.'

'Very well Dad, if that's how you feel and if you are sure you are up to it, the more the merrier. Now come on, drink up, I can see a car outside, it must be the Nixons and their mate they are earlier than expected. We must get a move on if we are to finish all this tonight.'

Albert and Ken locked the farmhouse door and walked into the farmyard to meet up with their fellow workers for the evening.

'Make sure you use those disinfectant footbaths chaps,' shouted Albert as they entered the farm yard.

'Don't worry Albert, we know the routine, we've been working on Billy Hill's farm yesterday. He's also been affected with this lot as have most of the farms around here as you know. It's a bloody shame,' retorted Geoff Nixon as he waded through the footbath.

At first, they all stood there motionless by the gate to the entrance to the fields and the remote barns. It was almost as if each of them didn't really want to go any further. This was one job they desperately didn't want to do. There was an eerie sort of silence in the air. It was just like another world out there. All around them it was silent, it was like a landscape with no life.

***

Saturday, 25th November 1967, 7.00pm

Jennifer was breathless when she finally arrived into work.

'Cutting it a bit fine aren't we Jennifer?' remarked her nightclub boss Nigel Simpson as he looked at his watch somewhat sarcastically. But Jennifer knew him well enough though not to take him seriously and she could already see the twinkle in his eye as he continued to fill the till with the money for the evenings float. Little did Jennifer know however that Nigel too had quite a crush on her but he still couldn't bring himself to asking her out on a date thinking she was well out of his league. Nigel was just a couple of years older than her and he would have loved to ask her out to meet up in the week for a drink but he simply couldn't cope with any rejection and the embarrassment in continuing to working together should she say no.

'Yeah, I'm awfully sorry Nigel, the bus was late I'm afraid. I'll make sure it doesn't happen again,' replied Jennifer who was now so out of breath she had to sit down for a minute.

'Don't you worry love, it'll be a while before the crowds arrive in this place, they'll be all crowding in down the pubs first I shouldn't wonder at this time and then taking the club by storm once it's gone nine o'clock. I tell you what though let's have a quick brew whilst it's quiet before the onslaught arrives. I'll make it, you look as though you could do with a cuppa and I bet you've also had a hard day working in the shop as well. Sit yourself down over there by the window, the bar is all prepared in any case, there's not that much to do at present.'

'Thanks Nigel, you're a star. I owe you one,' replied Jennifer as she hung her crimson full-length coat on the back of the office door. Office was too grand a word for it really, more a spare room with a desk. A room that always seemed to be piled to the ceiling with crates and boxes. She took a seat at a well-lit table in the corner of the bar and opened her handbag. She then used the opportunity to check and reapply her makeup and perfume after all it had been quite a rush leaving her flat in such a hurry. She failed to notice however that Nigel Simpson was eyeing her every move through a crack in the doorway.

***

Bear and Billet Public House, Chester, 7.15pm

The 17th century inn at the bottom of Lower Bridge Street was as busy as ever on the Saturday evening. The inn was one of the finest examples of a black and white half-timbered building which was once owned by the Earl of Shrewsbury. The billet as it became locally known was a very popular pub within the walled city and you had to be in there early doors if you had any chance of getting a seat on a Saturday evening. Most would use the pub however as their starting point before heading off to the various clubs in the city.

Heads turned and conversation suddenly stopped when the four stunning girls Anne, Sarah, Chris and Julie entered the pub. The girls just managed to grab the last table in the corner of the bar. Three of them were employed at the Shotton steelworks in the General Office typing pool and normally they would be out on the town a bit nearer home but tonight was a special night, they were celebrating Julie's 18th birthday. The plan was to have a few drinks and then move onto either the Clockwork Orange or the Quaintways nightclub. The decision had yet to be discussed and decided upon. Anne was out for a different reason she needed a good night out to try and help her forget all her recent troubles having been just made redundant.

'No news on the job front Anne?' asked Julie as she delved into her purse.

'No nothing yet but I'm optimistic, anyway Julie put that damn purse away. This is our treat tonight and don't argue with us,' said Anne, 'you are only eighteen once you know and we've all decided that us three will pay for the evening so you can just sit back and relax.'

'As relaxed as a newt,' giggled Julie as she lit up a cigarette.

'Erm no, not quite that relaxed,' laughed Sarah, 'We will however expect the same treatment on our birthdays of course. We've got a kitty going and we've decided we are treating you on your birthday. There is only one condition and that is just as long as you behave yourself,' said Sarah who was now on her feet about to get the drinks in.

'I can't promise that,' came the sharp reply, 'depends on who I might bump into.'

'Yes, we realise that and that's why we've set the condition! No honestly, you just enjoy the evening,' laughed Sarah as she made her way through the busy crowd to the front of the bar.

Sarah pushed her way through to the bar and almost immediately managed to catch the eye of the young barman who had just finished serving another customer.

'Four Babychams and one with a brandy please.'

She didn't wait to see if she was next in the queue, she had the attention of the barman and that was all that mattered to her.

Minutes later Sarah brought the tray of drinks over, placed them on the table in front of them and handed Julie the glass with the Brandy and Babycham.

'Here Julie, a large one for you and there's more of that to come!' exclaimed Sarah who was now placing the change back into the purse she was using for the kitty.

'Anyway Anne, isn't it your birthday soon,' said Julie, 'I bet your parents will be laying on a big party for you at their big posh house and I assume we'll all be invited?'

Anne was suddenly embarrassed and went bright red.

'Oh, sorry Anne, have I touched a nerve there?' said Julie.

'No, it's okay, you haven't heard, have you? My parents don't seem to want to have anything to do with me now. We had a huge row a few weeks ago and they kicked me out. I've moved out into a small bedsit in Shotton for the time being although I'm not looking forward to spending Christmas in there. I'm hoping to go and stay with my brother down south. I just hope I can find a job when I get back.'

Sarah and Chris remained silent throughout they already knew about Anne's predicament and had not mentioned it all to Julie.

'Oh, I'm awfully sorry Anne, I hadn't realised but I'm sure it will all work out in the end, you'll see.'

'Anyway, let's all toast Julie on her birthday,' said Sarah changing the subject and chinking the glasses.

'Never mind the drink I wouldn't mind more of that over there. Just look, he's gorgeous, I must say I quite fancy a bit of that,' whispered Julie looking over to a well-dressed boy who was standing on his own at the bar. The boy couldn't help noticing that he was being looked at by all four of them, smiled and nodded back returning their glances.

'Eh, fancy that, I think you've tapped on Julie!' exclaimed Chris as she took a mouthful of Babycham.

'Steady Julie, the night is as young as he is. He's probably still at school anyway! I mean just look at his haircut. I bet he had short pants on this morning and hasn't even started shaving yet. And when I say school it could be primary or secondary!' whispered Anne sarcastically.

'I don't care if he is still at school, he looks as fit as a butcher's dog to me,' laughed Julie, 'do you think I am still possibly too young to have a toyboy?'

They were too busy laughing and joking to notice the man in the corner who had been listening to every word they were discussing and he had now quietly slipped out of the side door.

Chapter 4

Saturday, 25th November 1967, 7.30pm

Albert and Ken together with Geoff and Owen Nixon accompanied by their mate Graham Hodgkinson made their way across the Mill House farmyard in the direction of the closed barn in readiness to prepare the cattle for slaughter. There was no urgency in their step as they opened the wooden five bar gate and then trudged across the muddy fields. This was not one of those tasks they had ever wanted to do and it was heart wrenching to watch. Ken had wanted to spare his dad from even being involved or seeing any of this but Albert wasn't having any of it. It was still his farm and he insisted on being involved at every stage. They had already placed the disinfectant footbaths around the barns and farm entrances. Ken slid open the huge barndoor and they entered the barn. They stood for a while in silence inside the barn almost reluctant to start the grim task which lay ahead of them.

'The vet will be here shortly,' said Albert, 'he said he was running late, bet he's been run off his feet with all the work they've got.'

'Right. I've discussed this with Dad everyone,' said Ken Smith, 'we have enough to do this weekend and our plan is to carry out the first of the slaughtering tonight and come back tomorrow evening at the same time. I assume everyone is available. We should be able to complete all the slaughtering by Sunday evening and then finish all the fires tomorrow. Is everyone agreed?'

They all nodded as the vet Bill Lyons appeared in the doorway.

'Come on, let's get on with it, there's no time to waste, the sooner we get started the better,' said Ken taking charge of the situation.

The vet opened up his bag and armed with a combination of injections and a gun they set about slaughtering the first of their livestock. Albert was heartbroken as one after another the carcasses were already starting to be piled high in one corner ready to be transported the following day to the bonfires in the adjacent field.

Suddenly without any warning Albert collapsed on the floor, he was breathless and holding his chest. He pulled himself up and sat down on a bale of hay near to the open doorway.

'Are you alright Dad, you look absolutely terrible?'

The vet and everyone else stopped what they were doing for a moment and waited for Albert to catch his breath.

'Yes, I'll be alright son,' panted Albert, 'It's no good Kenneth, I'm going to have to return to the farmhouse. I simply can't face this, it's just too much for me.'

'Ken put his arm around his dad's shoulder.

'I quite understand Dad, you take a rest. There's no hurry.'

'I'm afraid. It's soul destroying after all these years watching this happening. Can you possibly cope at all without me?' asked Albert who just couldn't watch it any longer.

'Yes of course we can Dad, you get back there to the house, we'll be fine here. The five of us can manage without you. Shall I walk you back to the house?' replied Ken who had wished he'd been far more forceful with his dad earlier on.

'No thanks Kenneth, I'll be fine. I'm not as young as I used to be.'

'I can't see why every animal has to be slaughtered,' continued Ken shaking his head, 'I mean in this day and age why can't it be dealt with by vaccination or something.'

'I agree son, but it's government policy. All the animals on the farm where an outbreak is confirmed have to be killed. We have no choice. I think the government department thinks vaccination would be too costly. Anyway, it's out of our hands now. I'll see you back at the farmhouse later on.'

'Get the kettle on Albert, we'll be quite parched after this lot!' shouted Owen Nixon who was trying in his own inimitable way to cheer old Albert up.

'Sorry chaps, I really thought I could deal with this but I just can't face it. It's just too much for me to watch.' replied Albert as he slid the barn door closed behind him. Albert was not one for crying but as he plodded his way across the muddy fields back towards the old farmhouse, he could feel a stream of tears running down his cheeks.

***

Saturday, 25th November 1967, 11.45pm

Taxi driver Bill Newton was getting towards the end of his shift and decided that he'd give it just another half an hour before finally heading home to his small two bedroomed semi-detached bungalow in Little Sutton near Ellesmere Port. He'd been on taxi duty since two o'clock that afternoon and he was now ready for home, he'd had a busy afternoon helping old ladies with their shopping but the evening had been so far relatively quiet. Bill was just approaching his 65th birthday and for most of his life he had worked as a plant technician at the nearby oil refinery. He'd taken voluntary redundancy however about ten years ago and most of his retirement lump sum had been quickly spent by his other half. Now after a long period of relaxation and overcoming an illness he had most recently resorted to become a taxi driver. Business had been unusually light for a Saturday evening and he'd just about had enough for the night.

Even though the taxi trade this evening had been quiet, Bill for once was actually quite glad to be in work, he'd split up from his wife a few months ago and the separation had gone very badly indeed. With Christmas coming just a month away Bill was preparing for the worst, a lonely Christmas either working or sat in front of the coal fire on his own. Pat Newton had been having an affair with one of Bill's old school mates of all people and he had found them in bed together one night when he'd returned home from work much earlier than expected. The rest was history, she'd now emptied what little money they had in their joint bank account, packed her bags and gone to live with her lover and his three children. Bill and Pat had had no children of their own and with Bill working odd hours he had no real friends or outside interests to speak of. He was now a broken man and was still trying to get over the break up. Faced with sitting in an empty house he'd decided he'd be far better off in work tonight and had requested the overtime; at least that way it would take his mind off the whole sorry saga.

He was now sat in his black cab with the heater full on, parked up alongside Chester cathedral. He'd finished the crossword and read every inch of the evening newspaper from front to back. As he sat there yawning his mind returned to the many good times the pair of them had had over the years, the caravan holidays they had on the Lleyn Peninsula in North Wales and recently more further afield on the Costa Brava in Spain. He kept thinking on the shame and how it had ended that way through her moment of sheer madness. He relieved the boredom by switching between Radio Luxembourg and the relatively new BBC Radio 1 station which was now gaining considerable popularity. As he sat listening to *"The Letter by the Box Tops",* he spotted a drunken youth come staggering from out of a side alley stumbling towards the cab from across the road. The lad looked to be in a bad way firstly even crossing the road was a challenge, almost zig zagging and completely oblivious to any traffic which fortunately there wasn't any. He tripped over the kerb, falling flat on his face. He shouted something to himself, Bill couldn't hear exactly what was said. As the youth got back on his feet with the aid of a nearby lamp post, Bill watched as the lad then vomited all down the front of his clothing. He stood there for a while propped up against the lamp post clinging onto it for dear life with his right hand and wiping his clothes down with his left hand. Minutes later the youth staggered back this time towards the car and after falling again this time face first onto the car bonnet he was now banging on the half-closed passenger's window.

'Is there any chance of a lift to Buckley mate? I'm in a bit of a hurry, gorra get up for work in the morning at the steelworks. I'll make it worth your while mate.'

Bill thought to himself, *Even if I was going in the direction of Buckley, I wouldn't let you in the car and certainly not with you in that state.*

'Sorry son, it's the wrong direction for me this time of night and in any case I'm on my way home soon, so why don't you try further down the street, you might find a cab down there that's going in that direction,' replied Bill as he quickly wound the window back up.

'Well, yer can stick yer taxi up yer arse then, what do I care. It probably wouldn't get me there anyway, it's a shit car. Probably wouldn't even get up the bloody hill.' shouted the youth who appeared now to be looking for something in the gutter to throw at the car.

The last thing Bill wanted at any time was a fight with a customer and particularly at this time of night. Much to his relief the youth disappeared as swiftly as he had arrived, this time down an adjacent alley way. Bill decided enough was enough for the night, he didn't wait for the youth to arrive back and immediately decided to call it a day and headed off back home.

***

Chester
Sunday, 26th November 1967, 12.35am

He could hear her breathing now as she got closer and closer. There was no one else about and the crowds had now dispersed. He waited for her to walk just past the alleyway and then his moment came. He stepped out immediately behind her. As quick as a flash before she had even time to look around and do anything, he'd already grabbed her from behind and forced her back down into the passageway against the brick wall. For one brief moment, he thought about stopping but then realised there really was no turning back now. This is it, his big moment. She struggled as she let out an enormous scream. 'Shut up, you bitch!' he shouted as she tried again to draw attention to anyone passing by but he was far too strong for her and held his hand tightly over her mouth restraining any chance of any further noise and with a violent blow to the head against the wall he knocked her unconscious. He reached into the small brown leather holdall and quickly applied a piece of duct tape across her mouth. He then tied her arms and legs up with the green heavy-duty twine that he'd also come equipped with. His hands were now covered in blood as she fell, limp landing in a heap onto the stone floor. He thought he heard footsteps and waited for a minute before checking if anyone was about. The cathedral clock signalled the 45-minute mark. It was quiet and then using all his strength he managed to drag her to his waiting car which was parked just around the corner. He quickly bundled her into the boot of the car and for now this phase of his plan was done, it had gone better than he had expected but, in his mind, he still had some unfinished business to deal with.

Chapter 5

Cheshire Constabulary HQ
Sunday, 26th November 1967, 2am

Detective Constable Nick Crowther was on the night shift and busy preparing a charge sheet in the CID office. He was all alone in the office, he hated the night shift and longed to get back on days but realised it had to be done if he was to have any chance of promotion. It had been a much quieter night than normal for a Saturday with only a couple of assaults early on in the evening which had been swiftly dealt with in the city centre. His boss was still dealing with an assault in Eastgate Street. He'd also had a stolen vehicle and a drunk & disorderly to deal with but apart from that it was quieter than normal. Nick had been spared working on the Foot and Mouth epidemic which had seen dozens of police officers including some of his own colleagues being drafted in to ensure that the farms were protected from unauthorised entry. It had shocked and saddened many people on how suddenly some of the farms had attracted unwanted visitors who were trying to get as close as possible to watching the many bonfires around the county.

Nick had been with the force joining as a cadet after leaving the Elfed Secondary Modern school in Buckley which was just over the border in North Wales. His father and grandfather had both been in the Police before him and he had been keen to follow in their footsteps. His dad had been with the Flintshire Constabulary and his grandad before that in the old Gwynedd force. Nick had shown great promise on one of the many investigative courses he had attended and had recently been transferred out of uniform into the CID department which was now based at the impressive new Police Headquarters that had just opened close to the city centre.

He had finally just finished typing up a charge sheet on the trusty old Brother deluxe typewriter which had certainly seen better days and looked out of place in the brand-new offices at HQ. He was just about to head off to the canteen for a brew and a spot of supper when he got a telephone call. He thought for an instance about leaving it and to let it go back to the switchboard but instead he raced back to his desk and picked up the receiver.

'Nick, it's Brian here down on the front desk, there's a gentleman down here who says he was walking home from the pub just down St Werburgh Street past the Cathedral earlier on and reckons that he's heard a loud scream coming from down one of the side streets. He went to have a look but he couldn't see or hear anything. I'm not aware of any other incidents this evening but he just thought we ought to know.'

'Thanks Brian, can you please take a few more details from him, it's probably nothing as I don't believe we've had any reported incidents over there. I'll follow it up later with the control room to see if they have been called at all and they can check it out with the beat officers in that sub-division. I'm just off for a well-earned cuppa now. I'm a bit parched after all that damn paperwork.'

'Okay, have a cuppa for me Nick, I'll take his details and bring them up to you later on.'

***

He eventually arrived back at the dilapidated cottage in the early hours of the morning and reversed the car down the old dirt track carefully trying to avoid the many potholes. It was difficult to even see the potholes in the dark and particularly after the recent heavy rainfall. He backed the car carefully into the old wooden garage which was just across the way from the cottage. As he stepped out of the car, he took a quick look around to see if anyone had seen him but he was at least half a mile from the nearest neighbour. It was pitch black and at that time of night he hoped they would all be safely tucked up in bed. He carefully closed the creaking wooden doors of the garage behind him and switched on the solitary light bulb that he'd managed to rig up from the house earlier the previous day. There was just enough light to work by, he didn't need much light and, in any case, it gave a sort of eerie but yet strange sort of cosy feel to the place. He took out and put on the grey balaclava from his inside pocket of his old wax jacket. He carefully opened the boot of the car and lifted the woman's body out. She was still limp and unconscious at this stage but as he moved her body, just then to his surprise, she started to open her eyes and immediately kicked out at him, missing his groin but hitting his left leg in the process. For one moment she thought she recognised those dark sunken eyes but his face was covered with the grey balaclava which had now been pulled down tight. She now struggled as best she could but she was helpless. She was bound tight and it was useless as he was far too strong for her. Her mouth was taped over and the green garden twine was now cutting deep into her wrists and ankles. He dragged her body as fast as he could across the concrete floor. She managed to kick off one of her shoes in the struggle, catching her ankle and badly bruising her in the process. He paused momentarily to catch his breath, all he could hear was her whimpering. He didn't care now and in fact he was well beyond caring. Limping across the garage he dragged her body further across the cold concrete floor to the workshop at the far end and using all the strength that he could muster he tied both of her arms up to the twisted six-inch nails that had previously been hammered into the rotting old oak beams. Both her legs were now bound together and fastened tight to a rusty old chain on the garage wall. She was completely helpless and everything in his mind so far had gone to plan, better in fact as he thought she would have put up more of a struggle. Slowly and carefully using a sharp knife from his old rusting metal toolbox he cut the sleeves off her coat followed by hacking it off completely. He stood back laughing, admiring his handy work and began now to rip into her blouse, tights and skirt. She suddenly got a waft of his dank stale breath as he moved even closer to her and she momentarily recalled his body odour, a mix of sweat and diesel oil. He could see the fear in her eyes now as she tried helplessly to kick out at him. She continued to scream but it was muffled and useless anyway in this remote location. He was now like an animal possessed with the anger and hatred that had built up inside him all those weeks. Nothing would stop him now, nothing and what's more he somehow began to actually enjoy it, in fact in the dark recesses of his mind he wondered why he had never done something like this before. But just as he was about to start tearing into her underwear he suddenly stopped. He could hear a faint noise in the distance, a car passing by, no it was coming down the dirt track towards the cottage. He quickly switched off the light and waited in the darkness. She desperately wanted to cry out for help but couldn't and she could now smell the foul stench of his bad breath. Suddenly it was quiet again, the car had gone and all she could hear was his heavy breathing in the darkness almost rasping.

Chapter 6

Blacon Police Station
Monday, 27th November 1967, 8am

PC Lewis and PC Morris had just returned to the back office following the usual morning briefing parade at the start of their day shift.

'Good morning Sarge and may I say what a lovely day to be in work. I must say you are looking exceptionally well this morning,' announced PC Lewis with a large grin on his face.

'No, you may not but thank you Lewis for your very kind thoughts,' replied the sergeant who was gathering a folder of charge sheets from the weekend.

'Do you know I was only saying to young Gareth here on a day like today it's an absolute pleasure to be here? A bit foggy out this morning but it's early yet. I'll tell you what it'll be nice when the fog lifts and to be out of this stuffy old office and on that open road again. I mean who was it who said a policeman's lot is not a happy one?'

'I think you'll find that was Gilbert & Sullivan; anyway, what's nice about it Lewis?' grumbled Sergeant White not looking up from the filing cabinet as he began starting to file the huge mound of paperwork in front of him which had been left over from the weekend.

PC Lewis loved to wind up the sergeant at any opportunity that he could. Most of the time it was taken as good healthy banter but at times and in particular at the start of the week the sergeant could be in a foul mood and this was just one of those days.

'I trust Sarge, we are on another routine beat patrol again today, back in the new patrol car again?' asked PC Lewis with a large grin on his face and rubbing his hands with glee.

'You are indeed Lewis and make sure you look after that new vehicle of ours, I don't want you coming back with some sob story saying you've pranged it otherwise you'll not just have me to explain to but you'll have the inspector to deal with,' said Sergeant White as he walked off towards the direction of the locker room.

'Oh, we will Sarge, we will,' winked PC Lewis to his colleague.

PC Gareth Morris and PC Peter Lewis had just taken over the brand-new Panda car that had been delivered and allocated to the Blacon police station. A brand-new shape Ford Anglia 105E with its large panels of white and duck egg blue. PC Morris and PC Lewis almost treated it as their own vehicle, well almost. The panda car had been seen by many UK forces as replacing the traditional "*bobby on the beat*". It was generally accepted that the rural and suburban areas could now be much more effectively patrolled by officers in these cars, as opposed to those on foot, bicycles, or even motorcycles and Cheshire were keen to follow their colleagues in other forces.

'I see Chalky is in one of his foul moods again, the miserable old git. Mind you I can't blame him being stuck in the office behind that damn typewriter all day, I'd be the same. At least we can get out on the open road again. Here you are Gazzer you can have a drive today, I can see you've been itching to get behind that wheel, let's get that car warmed up,' said PC Lewis as he tossed the keys across the desk to him.

'Hang on it is my bleeding turn anyway and you said yesterday…'

'Are you pair still here?' bellowed the sergeant returning from the locker room. 'Now out you go before I change my mind and put you back on walking the beat. I can always move you back onto that you know!'

'Yes Sarge, we are on our way,' came the reply in unison.

PC Lewis and PC Morris didn't wait for any further response and quickly made their way down the stairs and through into the car park. There parked at the side of the station was the new Ford Anglia patrol car with its American-influenced styling including that sweeping nose line which really looked the business.

'Now then, let's see how this beauty behaves on the straight,' said PC Morris has he climbed into the driver's seat.

'Steady, gazzer, we don't want the governor back on our case.'

'Just kidding mate, I'll take it easy, don't you worry.'

They had only been driving down the Sealand Road for about five minutes when PC Lewis received the call on their radio from the HQ control room.

'A2 from Sierra Oscar, are you anywhere near the Saughall Road?'

'Affirmative Sierra Oscar.'

'Mill House Farm, Saughall, the owner Mr Albert Smith has reported a body found in his fields. CID and the Pathologist have also been called to be in attendance. Over.'

'Yeah, received Sierra Oscar we are on our way. Over.'

'Body in the fields eh. Yes, I know where that farm is shouldn't take us too long to get there. Now we can really see what this thing will do. There is a nice long stretch along here,' said PC Morris as he switched on the blue light and put his foot to the floor sending the car roaring down the straight.

'Steady on Gareth,' shouted PC Lewis as the car hurtled towards a tight right-hand bend. There was a screech of tyres as they almost hit an oncoming lorry on the wrong side of the road.

'Get out of the sodding way you idiot!' shouted PC Morris waving his arm at the driver.

PC Lewis shut his eyes and waited for the inevitable crash.

'All under control, stop panicking, you can open your eyes now, he's moved over,' laughed PC Morris.

A few minutes later they arrived at the Mill House farm just ahead of the CID officers who had also been called to the scene. The first thing they noticed was the neatly trimmed hedgerows which had clearly been recently cut judging by the roadside debris. They parked the car at the entrance and were greeted initially by PC Kelvin Jones who was standing on farm protection duty at the closed five bar gate. The gate carried a large red and white warning sign stating

"Keep out – Foot and Mouth Disease".

'You can't go in there like that chaps.'

'Who can't, anyway like what, how would you like us to dress?'

'Look, can't you read it's a restricted area with foot and mouth. You'll need wellingtons and have to go through that disinfectant foot bath just inside the gate.'

'We can see that. By the way nice wellies Jonesy, they suit you, Army & Navy Stores or was it a bring-and-buy sale perhaps? Not my sort of colour but everyone to their own taste. Oh, come on, let us through,' said PC Lewis impatiently, 'we've been called out to the farmer, he's found a body in there apparently.'

'That's as maybe chaps but you can't come through here unless you first step through that bath of disinfectant and I can't see you doing that in those nice shiny clean boots of yours! It's more than my job's worth to let you through here. I've had strict instructions from up high. Orders is orders, you are not coming in and that's that.'

'Well, then we've had a bit of a wasted journey,' remarked PC Lewis turning to his fellow patrol officer. 'I'm sure the sergeant will love hearing this one. Hang on I tell you what, can you ask the owner to come to the entrance here as we need to speak with him? We'll stand here and make sure no one enters. Come on Jonesy, we can see you are equipped for it and you don't want to get into trouble with our sergeant now, do you?'

'Alright then, but you make sure no one comes through here or else I'll be in deep shit.'

'What deeper than normal Jonesy?' laughed PC Lewis as PC Jones returned two fingers back at him.

The two patrol officers stood at the gate of the entrance to the farmyard, there was still a strong acrid smell in the air from the burning of the animals over the weekend.

Minutes later PC Jones returned with Albert Smith the farm owner who was now looking very frail and was still in a state of shock after the discovery of the body.

'Ah, it's Mr Smith I believe, are you the owner of the farm?' asked PC Morris who had taken his notebook out in readiness.

'I am indeed Officer, we have never had anything like this before, I can tell you. This farm has been in my family for generations. You'd better come this way the field is over here. My son Kenneth found the body this morning we were just starting to clear the site after the fires from over the weekend.'

'I'm afraid we can't come in Mr Smith as we are not equipped as you can see,' remarked PC Lewis pointing down at his shoes. 'I'm sure you'll appreciate that but CID will be along in a moment and they will need to access the scene. I just need a few details from you before they arrive if that's alright?'

'Aye no problem.'

'So then what time did your son discover this body?' said PC Lewis who was also getting his notebook out in readiness.

'Let me see, I'd say it would be about 7.45 this morning sir, Kenneth and myself were the first into the fields this morning. He went on in front of me and he was the first to discover it. I was just starting the excavator up to clear up from the previous night's fires. When I got over there, I couldn't believe my eyes.'

'You say your son found the body and where exactly is your son now, Mr Smith?' replied PC Morris.

'He's clearing the other carcasses in the adjacent field.'

'Good grief how many have you found?'

'Animal carcasses you idiot,' whispered PC Lewis as he jabbed PC Morris in the ribs.

Just at that moment an unmarked police car pulled up outside the gate and DS Oldbury accompanied by DI Smethurst stepped out, green wellingtons in hand in readiness. They strolled over to the gate.

'Okay chaps, you can leave this to us now but before you go, what have we got here so far?' enquired DI Smethurst leaving his sergeant DS Oldbury to make any notes.

'Good morning, not a lot I'm afraid sir, this is Mr Smith the farm owner.'

Albert Smith nodded to the other officers.

'Good morning sir. You were saying Officer, so what do we know so far?'

'Well, as I say, not a great deal, the body was discovered at 7.45 this morning by Mr Smith's son Kenneth who I gather is working over there in the fields. As you can see, we haven't had access ourselves to the farm or the field but I can see that you've come equipped.'

'We have indeed. Right then, let's get over there. I suggest PC Lewis you stay here at the gate for the time being. We will probably need to call in extra resources, the pathologist and the forensic team have already been called out as far as I can gather,' said the DI as he donned his green wellingtons. Albert Smith led the two detectives through the gate and showed them the way through into the first field. They could see two JCB excavators in the distance still working in an adjacent field.

'I just hope those farmworkers have at least left the scene untouched,' said the DI pointing to the fields across the neatly trimmed hedgerows. As they approached the gate to the field in question Ken Smith who was driving one of the excavators had spotted them coming, stopped what he was doing and was already standing by the gate waiting for their arrival.

'Good morning, my name is Ken Smith thank you for coming over so quickly. The body is over here.'

The DI and DS both introduced themselves and followed Ken through into the next field.

DI Smethurst and DS Oldbury had both experienced several horrific scenes before when attending major incidents but nothing had prepared for them what they were now about to witness. They were shocked when they arrived at the still smouldering bonfire of animal carcasses in front of them, the smoke still drifting across the field. At first glance they hadn't noticed anything untoward but it was DI Smethurst who first caught sight of it. There in front of them was the charred remains of a human body, an open hand held out almost begging and crying out for help. Nearby were the remains of a discarded women's high heeled shoe which lay amongst the ashes.

'Right John, you get straight back to the farm to contact HQ immediately and ask them when we can expect the home office pathologist as a matter of urgency,' said DI Smethurst, 'we also need to protect this scene and set up an incident room. It needs to be as close as possible so I suggest it's probably best in Blacon police station if they have some space. You know the sort of office we need. Ask one of the officers to get the incident tent up as quickly as possible. In the meantime, I'll need to ask Mr Smith here a few more questions before I contact the Detective Chief Inspector on this one.'

'I'm straight onto it sir.'

Mr Smith, perhaps you would be good enough to allow me to use your phone?' replied DS Oldbury, 'I'll see you back at the farmhouse sir.'

Albert Smith grunted something and nodded for the DS to accompany him back to the farmhouse.

DS Oldbury and Albert Smith then made their way back across the fields to the farmhouse.

'How long will those men of yours be in the next field?' asked DI Smethurst now turning his attention back to Ken Smith.

'They are just at the start of their shift but they are almost finished now in that particular field, why do you ask?'

'Right, that's good, can you please ask them to stop what they are doing immediately and tell them I'll need to speak to each one of them back at the farmhouse. We will also need to protect this area. I don't want anyone other than the police and the forensic team here.'

'Well, can't they just finish off there is not much more to do over there?'

'Afraid not, I don't want anyone who is not directly involved in this investigation near this field, and I do mean anyone sir. I think you will be best advised to send them home sir, once I've spoken to each one of them of course.'

'Very well Officer. I'll get over to them straight away, in the meantime I'm sure my dad will give you every assistance back at the house,' replied Ken Smith who soon realised there could be no further work in the fields that day or for the very near future.

***

Norman Arrowsmith was in work early as usual to open up the grocery store and to sort out the daily newspapers before the rest of the staff came in at 8.00. Since his motorbike accident several years ago he'd had difficulty getting about but he always managed to be first in on time for 7am. It also gave him time to grab a spot of breakfast in the shop and have a quick glance at the morning papers before the morning rush. The first thing on his agenda however was making a brew for himself.

He was just reading through the headline story in the Daily Sketch announcing that the Beatles were planning to release their Magical Mystery Tour album in December when Joan Atkins who worked on the greengrocery counter came into the shop through the rear staff entrance.

'Good Morning Norman, it's not a bad old day, but it's a bit nippy this morning. Still as long as the snow keeps away, that's the main thing.'

Norman was so engrossed in the newspaper he hadn't even heard her arriving and jumped up quickly spilling most of his tea down the front of his brown overall.

'Good morning Joan, good grief is it that time already? I really must get a move on and open up the shop!' said Norman downing the remains of the mug of his tea quickly and trying desperately to wipe down his overall.

'No, actually I'm in a bit early today Norman, we have a delivery earlier than usual, the warehouse driver decided for some reason to start his round with us today. There's no hurry, I'll get the kettle on first, I'm sure you can manage another brew after spilling that one down yourself.'

'Thank heavens for that, but nevertheless I may as well open up now. Jennifer will be in here any minute,' said Norman reversing the close sign on the door, opening the blinds and unlocking the two heavy door bolts.

Almost as soon as the door had been opened the regular stream of clients came through to buy their usual cigarettes, newspapers, pies and sandwiches on their way to work. Norman was run off his feet and Joan had wondered why after 10 o'clock Jennifer still hadn't arrived into work. She knew Norman relied on her and he certainly could use that extra pair of hands.

'Norman, I'm really worried about Jennifer, it's not like her to be this late. If she missed her bus, then fine, I could understand that but this is unusual and she would have either called in or caught a later bus. Did she say anything to you on Saturday?'

'No, not a word.'

'Well, is there any chance you can go and see if she is alright. I'll look after the bacon counter for you while you are gone. I just wonder what's happened to her? The boss is due in to give us a visit later this morning but I can look after the place while you are gone.'

'Erm, yes, okay. I'll drive round to her place straight away and see if she is alright,' replied Norman as he took his overall off and hung it on the back of the storeroom door.

'Great thanks Norman, you get yourself off, the early morning rush is almost over now, I can easily cope here for the time being until you come back. I'll look after the place. Thinking about it she's probably feeling under the weather but best to be safe.'

Joan sat back for a minute and took a large swig of tea from the mug. She wondered if Jennifer had decided to take that short break she said she had badly needed, maybe she had gone to stay with her mother on Anglesey. She tried to think back to their conversation on the Saturday evening just as she had left the shop, perhaps she'd misheard her and she was actually taking a few days off after all. *Yes, that's it,* she thought, *she did say she was in need of a break, she's probably fine enjoying time with her mother on Anglesey.*

***

PC Lewis, PC Morris and PC Jones were now standing chatting at the farm entrance when a grey Volvo 144 saloon pulled up just outside the gate.

PC Lewis at first thought it was one of those nuisance sightseers who had attempted to get as close as possible to the foot and mouth farm scenes. The public and the police had been sickened by some of the individuals who had tried to get as close as possible to see the various livestock fires around the farm areas. He was about to ask the driver to politely turn around and leave the farm entrance immediately but as he marched over to the vehicle, he then recognised the familiar face of the local Home Office pathologist Dr Alan Scott.

'Good morning sir, I believe the DI is expecting you, he's over at the scene through there. You can leave the car there it will be fine. Oh, sorry sir, could I ask you please to use the disinfectant bath on your way through the farm yard?'

'Yes, of course thank you Officer, I do know the routine,' replied Dr Scott reaching into the boot of the car, grabbing his bag and donning a pair of green Barbour wellingtons.

'Yes of course, sorry sir, you'll find the DI through that farm gate.'

'Yes, thank you Officer.'

'What a nice bloke he is, you don't get many like him,' remarked PC Lewis as the pathologist made his way over to the field.

'You can leave this little lot to me now you know,' said PC Jones who was by now feeling like a bit of a spare part and thinking his job had been threatened somewhat with the arrival of the other two officers, 'I can deal with any access here you know, it doesn't need three of us.'

'Okay Jonesy, keep your hair on, we were only giving you a bit of support. It's all yours now, there is nothing more for us here,' responded PC Lewis we'll radio into the control room and tell them that we are now back on patrol.'

***

Norman Arrowsmith sat in the car at first for five minutes thinking a few things through, he had a lot on his mind at present. He thought about just saying he'd been to her flat and she wasn't in, perhaps just waiting for twenty minutes or so. In the end he decided to go around to Jennifer's flat. He started the engine and wasted no time at all in driving straight round to Jennifer's address. The traffic was light, all the works traffic to Broughton had finished earlier. He knew exactly where she lived, he'd even followed her home at one point and he had also given her a lift home on the odd occasion when they had been working late. He parked his old Morris Traveller car down a side road which was adjacent to the small three storey block of flats and then made his way towards the main entrance. His left knee was playing up more than usual this morning, funny he thought to himself how the cold weather affects it on some days or maybe it was the continuous bending down in the storeroom that has done it. As he limped down the gravel path, he could have sworn someone was watching him as a strange feeling suddenly came over him. He stopped momentarily and looked around but he could see no one, there was no one in sight. Everywhere was quiet with most people at work. He shook his head and continued on towards the building entrance. He was grateful that Jennifer lived on the ground floor as the stairs would have been quite a struggle for him today. As he entered the open lobby just outside her flat, he couldn't help noticing that her milk bottles from the last two days hadn't yet been taken in. He knocked several times and even shouted through the letterbox but there was no answer so he decided to walk round to the small garden at the back. He stepped across the wet lawn towards the flat's lounge window. He peered through the window and although the venetian blinds were still half shut, he could see there was no sign of life in there. He knew her mother came over every so often to stay for a weekend. He tapped on the window to see if anyone was in the lounge but received no response. He decided he needed to get back to the shop and realised he'd better get straight back there before the area manager arrived. As he got into the car to drive off, he hadn't noticed the curtains moving slightly in the window of the next door flat.

***

Blacon Police Station, Incident Room, 2pm

Events were now moving fast with Detective Chief Inspector Sheraton now being called in to take over in complete charge of the investigation as the SIO (*Senior Investigating Officer*) on the Saughall case now known as Operation Ulysses. Michael Rudyard Sheraton was head of the divisional CID based at HQ and he had served the force for just over twenty-nine years. Like Rudyard Kipling his parents had also named him after the small village near the reservoir close to Leek in Staffordshire. As a small child he had been a frequent visitor to the delightful village where his grandparents had once lived. As unusual as his middle name was, he was always grateful that he hadn't been named after one of the other reservoirs in the area! Now looking forward to his retirement which was just months away he was hoping for an easier life but it wasn't to be. Sheraton was well thought of in the force having worked in many murder investigations since initially moving into CID as a Detective Constable and working his way through the ranks. The Detective Chief Inspector had just attended the post-mortem and drove immediately over to the Blacon police station where DS Oldbury had already established the incident room. The room had been previously used as a combined briefing and rest room and consisted of an assortment of desks, old chairs and typewriters. It looked more like an antique auction room than a police major incident room. It was not ideal with limited desk space and a lack of phones but the incident team just had to make the best of it. With no dedicated major incident rooms in the force they were quite used to working wherever they could, church halls, school rooms, canteens and in one recent case even a cricket pavilion with no phones whatsoever. On one wall was a large cork noticeboard which had been previously used in the past to inform officers and civilian staff of both forthcoming social events together with the station's monthly duty rosters. These notices had all now been removed and in their place was a small collection of photographs pinned to the board relating to the incident location together with an ordnance survey map of the area. A large empty carousel wheel which would eventually hold all the manual cards was situated on a desk in the far-right hand corner. DS Oldbury had done well in such a short time to pull together the team and the actual incident room.

Detective Chief Inspector Sheraton found himself a vacant desk and had already started to prepare a few notes to address the incident investigation team that had just been assembled before him. The DCI left nothing to chance and always made notes in preparation for any meeting. After ten minutes he called the officers to attention.

'Right chaps, now if you can just stop what you are doing. Can I just have your attention for just for a few minutes. I have just returned from the post-mortem with Dr Scott and this is what we know so far and I'm afraid there isn't a great deal that I can tell you at this stage of the investigation. Nevertheless this is what we have so far. We have an unidentified female body, probable age between 18 to 25 of which we are currently awaiting the pathologist's post-mortem initial report but I expect to receive this report tomorrow morning at the latest. At least that's what Dr Scott told me as I left and he normally sticks to his word. According to the farm owner Mr Albert Smith the foot and mouth fire that she was found at in fields on Mill House Farm, Saughall had been lit at approximately 11.15pm on the Sunday night. Albert Smith, his son Kenneth, their vet and three farm workers were busy dealing with the foot and mouth incident at their farm.'

'They had several fires to deal with that weekend and this was one of the last ones to be lit apparently. After the last fire had been lit, the farmworkers involved then finished for the evening and went home. Albert Smith retired to bed and his son Kenneth Smith stayed up having a nightcap before retiring. They left the fires burning and went home for the night and we believe therefore judging by the state of the body she must have been dropped there between the hours of midnight and seven o'clock on the Monday morning. Judging by the state of the body however we believe she was murdered elsewhere and the body had been dumped into the fire.'

'We expect the pathologist to confirm this when we get his report. Kenneth Smith, the son of the owner of Mill House Farm who was the first person to notice the body says when he visually inspected the bonfires on the Monday morning in the early hours they were still smouldering and he says that at first, he didn't notice anything untoward. He first noticed the remains of a lady's shoe on the edge of the ashes and at closer investigation, then saw the remains of the body.'

'The body could of course have been dropped there on the Sunday evening prior to the bonfire being lit but I think it's highly unlikely as the farmworkers would have still been working in the fields. So we now need to allocate the roles on this investigation. DI Smethurst, I want you to be our office manager here so can you also please as a matter of priority start setting out the sequence of events chart across that back wall, oh and make sure that you include the entire weekends significant entries leading up to this. At this stage we will need to record and consider every little thing, dates, times, sightings, every movement, parked cars etc. I mean everything, is that understood?'

'Certainly sir,' replied DI Smethurst who was well versed in the force incident room procedures having worked on several incidents in the past and certainly knew the importance of capturing all the information regardless of relevance at this stage.

'John, I want you to take charge of the card indexing as and when we get any information. We don't have much to go on at present but we do have to make a start somewhere. You can start with the witness statements that DI Smethurst took from the Smiths, the vet and the farm workers earlier on. They are being typed up at present downstairs but you should have them anytime. I'm afraid you will also have to mark these up for indexing as soon as possible until DS Bradshaw helps you to take this task over.'

'No problem sir,' replied DC John Blackwell and didn't bother waiting for the end of the briefing. He immediately sat down at the corner desk, making himself as comfortable as possible behind the large carousel wheel of blank cards. He first set about underlining some of the text in the incident logs from the control room and then began the laborious process of hand writing this information onto the cards, the cards which would hopefully be used to provide the answers to their main queries. Even though at this stage they had only six witness statements together with a couple of vehicle sightings John Blackwell would already have his hands full in cross indexing the information they had so far gleaned.

'DC Johnson, isn't it? I gather you've just joined CID is that right?' enquired the Detective Chief Inspector as he looked up from his notes.

'Yes sir,' replied Peter Johnson almost standing to attention.

Peter Johnson was the new boy to the Blacon Police station having just been transferred from the traffic division and he was still finding his feet in CID.

'Good afternoon, welcome on-board lad. I am sure everyone has made you welcome, I think you'll find this section of the force a bit different from what you are used to but I'm sure you'll enjoy it. Now I want you to immediately check with missing persons in force HQ and to also follow up on those vehicle sightings, someone must have seen something unusual. See what you can find, you can get together with DS Bradshaw on that one.'

'Yes sir, certainly sir,' replied DC Johnson eagerly.

'DS Bradshaw.'

'Yes sir.'

'As I mentioned I want you to be responsible for reading all the information that comes into the incident room and to raise any officer actions, interviews etc anything you think that we will need to follow up on. I'll need to review all of these with you of course on a daily basis. Anything you think could be especially important or unusual can you please make a separate note of it on the noticeboard and we can decide at our morning meetings on whether it's worth pursuing or not. Now if you don't mind gentlemen I need to get back and also clear my desk of my other case work so if there are no questions, I'll head off back to the HQ?'

'Yes sir, I have just the one, do we know how old this girl was?' piped up DS Bradshaw who had been busy making notes throughout the DCI's briefing and had somehow missed the DCI's previous comment on the probable age of the victim.

'It's too early to say yet, as I say we estimate she was between 18 and 25 but we'll have to wait for the pathologist's report to confirm that. Well, in the meantime gents, if there are no further questions, I'm off first to see the pathologist and then heading back to Police HQ to also prepare for a press briefing. I'm planning to be back here tomorrow morning first thing to go through everything we have so far. Ring me at my desk if we have any developments whatsoever, Helen my secretary will take any messages.'

Chapter 7

Blacon Incident Room
Tuesday, 28th November 1967, 9am

'Good morning, Major Incident room, DS Bradshaw speaking, how can I be of help?'

'Oh, good morning, is that the murder incident room?' said the croaky voice on the end of the telephone.

'It is, can I help you sir?'

'Yes, I'm ringing about that body that was discovered in that fire yesterday morning over in Saughall. My name is Owen Nixon. I was one of the farm workers at Mill House Farm on the Sunday evening you see. I did give a statement to one of your officers at the farm yesterday morning but we were all in shock, I mean very nasty business that. I can't just remember his name, now what was it again? Smethwick, Smedley or something like that anyway.'

'That would probably be DI Smethurst sir, he's not here at the moment so how can I be of assistance?' repeated DS Bradshaw.

'Aye that's him, DI Smethurst, nice bloke, seen him before somewhere, can't think where. Well, he told me that if I can remember anything else, I should contact the incident room straight away and it was only after giving my statement,

I remembered something which might be relevant. After I got home late on the Sunday night when we had finished setting the fires at the farm, I remembered something that I think may be of interest or of course it's maybe nothing at all. I mean you never know do you with these things? I would hate to be accused of wasting police time, anyway I realise that you have to consider everything and some of it might just be pure coincidence I suppose. I mean these things happen and you do read these stories of…'

'Yes, yes, please go on sir,' interrupted DS Bradshaw who was trying his level best to be patient but was keen for Owen Nixon to get straight to the point.

'It's like this you see I live about five miles away from the Mill House farm near Shotwick and I was heading home and I couldn't help noticing a car with no lights on parked at the side of the road, actually it was on a grass verge as there is no layby there. As I got nearer the driver seemed to slip down in his seat out of sight as if he or she didn't want me to see them or that's what it looked like anyway to me. I mean it could have been a couple of lovers up to no good if you get my drift. As I say I don't know if this is relevant or just purely co–'

'So whereabouts was this sir?'

'It was on erm, damn, what's it called now, I drive past there every day, what's it called? Erm, Lodge Lane, aye, that's it, Lodge Lane. I always takes a short cut, see, back home, you see. I can't remember the exact spot as it was dark of course and the road was unlit. There's a ditch on one side of the road and this ere car was on the opposite side, half on the road and half on the grass verge. I almost ran into it and I hadn't had a drink. Bloody stupid place to park if you ask me, it's a wonder I didn't hit it.'

'And can you remember the make or the type of car?'

'Ooh, now let me think, no, you've got me there Officer. No, it was far too dark to see, it was a dark coloured car I think, probably an older one. Not good on cars I'm afraid. Afraid that's all I can recall.'

'Well, thank you for that sir, we do appreciate your phone call. If anything else springs to mind, then please don't hesitate to call us on this number.'

Just as the DC had finished the phone call and replaced the receiver in came DCI Sheraton this time accompanied by DI Smethurst.

'Good Morning all,' shouted the Detective Chief Inspector, 'I don't suppose there is any news on the pathologist's report yet?'

'Nothing as yet,' replied DS Bradshaw, 'shall I chase it up sir?'

'Damn it, I was hoping we would have had that by now. No, I'll call Dr Scott myself later, he's normally on time with this sort of thing, he's perhaps been called out to another job. Now can you all stop what you are doing for a moment, we just need a quick review on where we're at together with a new development you may not be aware of. Firstly, the forensic team at the scene have recovered a small amount of jewellery found at the edge of the fire. These are a woman's Sekonda gold watch and a gold-plated charm bracelet. I don't want to release this information yet to the public. DS Bradshaw I would like you to try and find out more information on the lady's shoe that was found in the ashes, make, size, where it was likely to have been bought etc if possible and also find out what you can on the watch and bracelet. Whoever did this was clearly not interested in the jewellery. The back of the watch by the way has a heart with a brief inscription *"J & N always in my heart"*.

'Yes sir, certainly sir.'

'Secondly the vehicle sightings in the area, I gather we now have a few more details of these, one of which is a dark coloured car which was parked in a layby outside the Saughall village and an old grey Morris minor sighted not far from the entrance of Mill House farm. Both of these are in the early hours of Monday morning. Have we identified these yet DC Johnson?'

'Afraid not sir, the information we had on those two was very sketchy to say the least but I'm still working on it.'

'Good, well keep on with that, someone must have seen something out of the ordinary in that area. DI Smethurst can you please organise a house to house in the area, I realise it's mainly farm buildings but there are a few farm cottages close to the scene. They may have seen something out of the ordinary, I suggest…'

'Sorry to interrupt sir but I've also taken a phone call just before you came in from one of the farmworkers who says he saw a suspicious vehicle in Lodge Lane just minutes from the farm. Says his name was Owen Nixon one of the local farm workers, he said he has already given a statement.' responded DS Bradshaw who was still writing the details from the call down on the scrap pad.

'Interesting, yes, I remember having sight of the Nixon statements. Two brothers as I recall. Jot down his contact details and let me have a copy again of his statement. I'd quite like someone to visit Mr Nixon sometime, once he has had time to think he might be able to provide us with a bit more information on that car. Look I'm in a hurry as I'm late for another meeting. I must head back to HQ to give old Duckworth an update, he's been pestering me. I imagine the chief has also been onto him by now.'

***

Blacon Police Station
Tuesday, 28th November 1967, 10.15am

'Can I speak to the senior officer please?'

'I'm sorry Madam the Detective Chief Inspector is out of the office at present, perhaps I can be of assistance?' replied DC Johnson politely.

'Well Officer, I am ringing about a neighbour of mine who I haven't seen since the weekend and I'm somewhat concerned. It maybe of course she has gone off for a short break but I am sure she would have told me and the milk bottles are still being delivered to her flat.'

'Really madam, let me start by taking down a few details, firstly what's your name?'

'It's Edith Flowers.'

'And your address?'

'Flat 2, Hawthorn Avenue, Saltney.'

'And your neighbour Mrs Flowers?'

'What about her?'

'Her name, your neighbour, the one you are calling about, the one you are afraid is missing?'

'Oh right. Yes, sorry, I'm Miss Flowers actually. Yes, my neighbour is Jennifer Webb from Flat 3. She's a lovely girl and I hope she hasn't come to any harm at all. I've been worried sick, I've not slept all night. You see it's not like her to just go off without letting me know.'

'Right, well thank you Miss Flowers, we'll look into this and get back to you. We will probably need to come and see you for a statement but in the meantime is there anything else that I can help you with?'

'No, I don't think so. Oh, yes, yes, there was something else a strange man yesterday came down the path to the flats, he looked very shifty, bit scruffy to me had a bit of a limp. Never seen him before and of course he might have been visiting one of the other tenants. He wasn't there long but was snooping about looking through the window.'

'Well, thanks for that Miss Flowers, please don't hesitate to contact us if you have any further information or if Miss Webb turns up. She might have gone away for a long weekend perhaps.'

'Yes, it's possible of course. Thank you.'

As DC Johnson replaced the receiver, he thought for a minute and then proceeded to write out two nominal cards with the information that he'd just been given.

***

DCI Sheraton arrived back at Police HQ and made his way up the stairs to the CID floor, he was just in time to see ACC Duckworth who was about to go into his office after he'd just had his morning meeting with the chief constable.

'Ah Michael, just the very man, come into the office and take a seat. I was about to ring you, I thought you would still be back at Blacon. The chief has been asking me for an update on that Saughall case. I couldn't tell him much, so what do we have so far?' The ACC pulled up his chair and the DCI took a seat at the small conference table adjacent to the ACC's desk.

'Well sir, there is not much additional information that I can provide you with at present. We are really awaiting the results of the post mortem from Dr Scott. We expect those anytime. We haven't as yet identified the body. We do have a few leads at present which we are following up but we've drawn a blank so far on the missing persons.'

The Detective Chief Inspector didn't want to release the jewellery information just yet and decided to keep that from the ACC who he believed based on the past had a nasty habit of releasing certain pieces of information by accident to the public.

'Right well as soon as you get something concrete let me know,' replied the ACC as he rose from his desk indicating the meeting was now over and was just about to leave the office.

'Actually, there was something else sir?' said DCI Sheraton as they both entered the corridor.

'And what was that?' replied the ACC as he turned around sharply.

Michael Sheraton suddenly wondered whether this really was the right moment to tell the ACC about his planned retirement and instead he quickly changed his mind.

'Oh, nothing sir, it will wait for now. It's not that important, I will keep you posted.'

The ACC looked puzzled for a moment, shook his head and started down the stairs.

The Detective Chief Inspector thought this really wasn't the right time to talk about retirement and certainly not in the corridor with people passing by every minute. He entered his own office across the way and sat for a short while contemplating his phone call before finally picking up the receiver and dialling Dr Scott.

'Good morning Alan, this is Michael Sheraton at Police HQ, do we have any news yet on the Saughall incident?'
'Ah good morning Mike, you must be psychic I was just about to ring you. Yes, we've completed the report and I'll send it over straight away, you should get it no later than lunchtime today but just to give you a quick summary while you are on the phone…'

Chapter 8

Blacon Police Station
Tuesday, 28th November 1967, 3.15pm

Detective Chief Inspector Sheraton had now read through the pathologist's report in detail and was shocked to read its entire contents. He now had the task of briefing the major incident team at Blacon and to catch up on any further developments whilst he'd been out of the office. He drove straight over to Blacon however the traffic in the city centre was heavier than normal with unexpected road works and a diversion in operation on the Western Avenue which led to him being late. Twenty minutes later he parked up and made his way upstairs to the incident room.

The Operation Ulysses incident room was buzzing when the DCI arrived. Temporary additional phone lines had now been installed and following appeals on local radio they had already been inundated with numerous calls from the public. The back log on manual card indexing all of this information was already starting to build up fast.

The DCI found himself a desk in the corner, sat down and thought through the information they had already gleaned. He started to prepare the policy log in front of him.

He'd only been seated for about a minute when DC Johnson emerged with a tray full of teas.

'I'm sorry sir, I didn't see you come in, can I get you one?'

'No thanks Peter, I've drunk enough tea for today, I don't suppose you've got a beer in the kitchen?'

'I can have a look sir…'

'I'm just joking Peter, you carry on.'

'Actually sir. I'm glad that I've caught you,' said DC Johnson as he placed the tray of mugs on the desk at the side. 'I've just had Albert Smith the farmer from Mill House Farm on the phone he wants to know when they can continue with destroying their livestock. He said he knows it's early days for the investigation but it's important that with the foot and mouth epidemic they continue as soon as possible. I said I'd get back to him as soon as I knew anything.'

'Ah right, yes, I'd forgotten about the Smiths. Well, as long as they keep out of the incident field for the time being Johnson, they should be okay to continue. Give Mr Smith a call will you and check that the entire field is marked off and completely out of bounds. I don't what anyone in there.'

'Will do sir, I'll ring him back in a minute.'

The DCI then signalled to everyone that he wanted their attention and waited for a suitable opportunity to address the team.

'Good afternoon, we now have Dr Scott's initial report and it doesn't make for good reading I'm afraid. We have no formal identification as yet, the body which was badly burnt is that of a girl aged between eighteen and twenty-five years of age. It looks as though we will need dental records to make any formal identification. The report also goes onto say that the victim had suffered multiple broken bones and a fractured jaw. I don't need to tell you that this girl had gone through hell and I'm more determined than ever to find the bastard who did this to her. You will all notice that we now have an Ordnance Survey map on the far wall, make sure you all get familiar with this. DC Blackwell has marked on the map the location of the fire, the farm and the surrounding lanes. There is no doubt in my mind that this bastard must have carried her body across the field, apart from the excavators there are no tyre marks as such or footprints, so whoever did it must have been strong. There is a gate just fifty yards away leading to a single-track lane which joins up with the main road. It's possible he or she took that route to dump the body but it's anyone's guess where she was murdered in the first place.'

***

Cestrian Radio
Wednesday, 29th November 1967

A spokesperson said: "Cheshire Police can confirm that a Post Mortem has now been conducted after the charred remains of a girl's body was found at Mill House farm near Saughall on Monday morning 27th November.

The girl has not yet been identified but she is believed to have been between 18 and 25 years of age.

The investigation is ongoing and anyone who witnessed any suspicious activity in the Saughall area during the last few days or even weeks, or has any knowledge of the incident is asked to contact the police at Blacon Police Station as soon as possible."

***

Wednesday, 29th November 1967, 7.00am

The events of the weekend had been bothering him so much that it was keeping him awake at night. It had all gone to plan just as he had worked out but he didn't want to leave anything to chance and decided he would have no option but to make the trip and re-visit the old cottage again to return to the wooden garage to remove any possible evidence. He waited until it was almost day light and drove back down the dirt track. There was no one about, it was still early as he parked the car this time behind some trees about half a mile from the old derelict stone cottage and walked across the yard to the wooden garage. He thought for a minute about whether to just simply burn the entire place down completely and destroy the damn garage but although it would be easier realised that it would certainly draw attention. He had come equipped as usual and decided to continue with his plan. He collected the remains of the ripped clothing that was lying around the garage floor and stuffed it all into a hessian bag that he'd brought with him. There were still traces of blood splattered across the workbench and floor. Once he'd cleared up, he decided to disinfect everywhere as he wasn't going to leave anything to chance. He'd just finished cleaning the floor and was about to close the garage door behind him when he heard a car approaching in the distance. He hid down behind the workbench and could just see through the dusty broken window, a car turning off the main road and then to his horror he noticed it was actually coming down the old dirt track towards the old cottage. He crawled across the floor on his hands and knees quickly bolting the garage doors from the inside. He crouched further down as the car got closer and closer finally coming to a halt directly in front of the garage. He could now hear two voices but it was muffled and couldn't hear what each of them was saying. The strong smell of disinfectant had now got to his throat and he desperately wanted to cough but he held the handkerchief over his mouth and nose. He could now hear footsteps moving slowly away from the garage in the direction of the derelict cottage. Minutes later he could hear them coming back. They tried rattling the garage doors and then the next thing he heard was two doors slamming and the car reversing back down the dirt track. He looked at his watch and it was now just after 8.30am, it was time for him to put the final phase of his plan into action.

Chapter 9

Evening Post
Friday, 1st December 1967

A woman's badly burned body has been found on Monday morning 27th November at Mill House Farm, Saughall according to the Cheshire Constabulary.

Detectives believe that the unidentified victim was killed elsewhere and that her body was later dumped amongst burning animal carcases.

The victim is believed to have been between 18 and 25, according to the senior investigating officer Detective Chief Inspector Michael Sheraton at Cheshire CID.

The body was found by farmer Kenneth Smith who was clearing up after the previous night's foot and mouth fires according to the police. Detective Chief Inspector Sheraton said that checks on missing persons are ongoing and at least two suspect vehicles had been spotted in the area, but at this stage they have no further descriptions. The Police are currently awaiting the results of the post-mortem examination.

Officers are particularly keen to trace the movements of vehicles on the Sealand Road late on the Sunday evening 26th November.

And police want to speak to anyone who spotted anything odd or out of place within that timeframe in the Saughall area.

Anyone with any information is please asked to contact the major incident room at Blacon Police Station.

***

Detective Chief Inspector Sheraton was up bright and early on the Friday morning, in fact he too had a job sleeping and he simply couldn't get the case out of his mind. With a teenage daughter himself he was clearly visibly shaken at the entire incident. He was keen to get into work, took a quick shower and didn't even bother with breakfast. He decided to head straight to the incident room at Blacon police station instead of going via HQ. He knew if he went to his office he could be delayed with other investigative matters. On arrival he was greeted in the car park by the now familiar face of DS Bradshaw who was just about to get in his vehicle.

'You're in early Bradshaw, are you off somewhere? Are you going to be long as I could really do with a chat with you when you come back?'

'Good morning sir, yes, I shouldn't be too long I'm just off to interview that lady in Saughall. Mrs Matthews. Apparently, she reported a suspicious vehicle matching one of the two descriptions we had. She heard it reported on the local radio yesterday, anyway I should be back later all being well to follow up on that jewellery that was found at the fire.'

'Good, well give me a call later on if I'm not in the incident room. Don't forget to let me know how you get on.'

'Will do sir.'

The Detective Chief Inspector made his way through the station rear entrance and pounded up the stairs two at a time to the incident room. Already displayed on one of the walls of the incident room were a number of photographs of the scene together with a large ordnance survey map of the area. The photographs of the charred body were not for general viewing in the incident room and these were being kept for the time being in a folder in a drawer in the SIO's desk.

DI Smethurst was busy adding to the rough timeline of the known events across one of the walls using an old roll of wallpaper. 'Morning sir, I didn't hear you come in,' said DI Smethurst as he stepped down off the chair he was balancing on.

'You've timed it just right sir, I've almost finished here. It's not much as you can see but I'm afraid it's all we've got at present.'

The two detectives stood back and gazed at the handwritten timeline for a brief moment.

'Yes, you're right, it's not much at present but hopefully today we can at least put some flesh on the bones if you pardon my inappropriate pun.'

'Indeed. Do you fancy a brew before you start sir?'

'I will indeed, coffee please white no sugar. I've not had any time for breakfast this morning and I'll try and get something to eat in the canteen a bit later on but I'm keen to get started on this lot first.'

'Yes, it's a strange one this sir, I remember a case over in Tarporley that I worked on a few years back when someone tried to destroy all possible evidence by burning the body, they even set light to the surrounding barns but whoever did this one was either disturbed during the process or even stranger somehow still wanted her to be found.'

'Disturbed, is the right word, whoever did it was a right bloody animal.'

'I agree. I don't suppose we have any idea on who she was yet sir?

'No not at all, we are still checking the missing person records from outside the area. We have had a few early enquiries from members of the public which we are following up.'

'I'm keen that we follow up as quickly as possible the other leads we have had, for example that lady who reported her neighbour missing, the one in Saltney, what was her name again?'

'Ah, Miss Flowers, yes, a nice old lady, I'll get someone over to speak to her as soon as possible sir.'

***

DS Jim Bradshaw followed the rough directions that he'd been given back at the police station but he was now well and truly lost. He was in his grey Austin A40 in the middle of nowhere, down a country lane and he was now having to trace his way back to one of the landmarks that he'd been given back at Blacon. Having recently transferred from the West Riding Constabulary to the Cheshire Constabulary he was still getting to grips with the local area. The directions he'd been handed were sparse to say the least and he was just at the point of getting out of the car and walking the rest of the way but in reality, he had no idea on the remaining distance to the address that he'd been given. He decided he had no option but to ask someone for directions, but there was simply no one in sight. He sat there for a few minutes checking and double checking the very sketchy handwritten directions that he'd been given. Suddenly coming towards him without warning from around the next bend accompanied by a cloud of black smoke came an old Massey Ferguson tractor and trailer. Jim quickly wound down the car window down and waved the tractor driver to stop.

'Excuse me sir, I'm sorry to trouble you but I wonder if you can help me, I am looking for Riverside Cottages, Riverside Lane.'

'Now, let me think,' replied the driver as he removed his moth-eaten cap revealing a thick head of unruly grey hair and scratching his head in the process. 'Ah yes, that would be Jack Hill's old place. That would be back there about a mile on your left. You must have missed the first turning into Chamber's Lane. It's no more than a dirt track. Follow that road down there for about half a mile and I think you'll find Riverside is on the right or at least it was the last time I looked.'

Jim Bradshaw couldn't get over how the old man's badly fitting dentures moved around in his mouth almost out of control at times whenever he spoke, they seemed to have a mind of their own. He thanked the old man and managed to turn the car around in the narrow lane. Minutes later he was following a tree lined dirt track which was completely overgrown with rough grass verges on each side of the lane. The branches from the bushes were now scratching the windows of the car as he drove carefully at the same time trying to avoid the numerous potholes. As he rounded a long sweeping bend a pair of whitewashed cottages came into view. The cottages which were badly in need of painting looked as though they had been previously used to house farm labourers as part of a possible farming estate. Both cottages looked drab as though they could do with some attention and one of them with slates missing off the roof in particular looked as though it was now completely derelict.

There was nowhere to park and Jim had no option but to try and park his car on a rough grass verge across the lane from the cottages. It was dark and gloomy with heavy rain clouds in the distance. As he got out of the car, he checked the faded name on the old wooden gate, he could just about make it out, "Rose Cottage". The paintwork on the gate was chipped and peeling with rusty hinges just about holding it together. He was in the right place alright, the adjoining cottage with grimy windows and no curtains looked completely desolate. He lifted the latch of the wooden gate which squealed open and made his way down the overgrown brick path leading to the front door. A crumbling wooden porch, badly in need of repair surrounded the rotting doorway. The remains of what looked to have been out of control climbing roses and suckers clung onto the broken trellis work. He was just about to knock on the door when a large black cat scurried out in front of him, almost knocking him off his feet and taking him by complete surprise. He knocked on the door and waited patiently. Nothing but silence, there was no response, he knocked again and this time shouted through the cobweb strewn letter box. After a few minutes he decided he'd had a wasted journey and started walking back down the path. He was about to open the gate when a voice from nowhere shouted out to him.

'Whatever it is, we don't want any,' cried the voice.

He looked back and couldn't see where the voice was coming from.

'So be off with you and shut the damn gate behind you, else I'll set the dog on you,' boomed the voice again.

Jim still couldn't work out where the voice was coming from but started walking back to the house. It was only then as he looked up, he noticed a little old lady leaning out of a tiny window in one of the tiny attic rooms.

'I'm DS Bradshaw, Miss Matthews,' he shouted, 'you spoke to our incident room staff the other day about a vehicle sighting. I'd just like to have a quick chat.'

'You've done what with the cat?'

'Nothing with the cat. I'm DS Bradshaw.'

'DS what?'

'DS Bradshaw from the Cheshire Constabulary.'

'Oh right, I thought I'd given you all that information on the phone. Hang on there, I'll be down there as soon as I can.'

Jim Bradshaw stood waiting patiently at the front door and eventually after several minutes had passed Miss Matthews arrived downstairs and attempted to yank open the creaking front door. The oak door was badly swollen and seemed to be wedged somehow on the stone floor. Jim gave it a helpful push nearly knocking the old lady off her balance in the process.

'Come on in, Officer, I'm sorry about that. I thought you were trying to sell me something, I was upstairs having a bit of a tidy up. By the way I haven't got a dog but you can't be too careful these days.'

Jim entered the front room cottage which was like something out of a museum. It was like stepping back in time and the place stank of an odd mixture of cats and damp. In fact, he immediately thought of the similarity with Miss Matthews and Miss Havisham in Great Expectations. Cobwebs were strewn across old rotting furniture. Some of the furniture had been covered over with old sheets and newspapers. An old coal fire which had seen better days was burning silently in the hearth and providing very little heat.

'So sit yourself down love, make yourself comfortable,' said Miss Matthews as she gingerly moved about the front room and eventually took her seat in an old wooden rocking chair.'

Jim continued to stand and thought to himself that he could have sworn the rocking chair was already moving when he first entered the cottage or was it just his imagination.

'Now before we start Officer, will you have a cup of tea?'

'No thanks Miss Matthews, I've only just had one,' he lied. He thought to himself, *There is no way I'm partaking of any light refreshments in this dirty old place.*

'Now then, come on in, sit yourself down love, there's no charge and I won't bite you.'

Jim looked around trying to find somewhere vaguely clean to take a seat. He pulled up an old rickety dining chair a bit nearer the fire which was providing very little heat into the small front room.

'So, let me get this right. We understand from your phone call Miss Matthews that you saw a car pull up on the lane outside your cottage the other Sunday night, is that correct?'

'Yes, I had to walk to the phone box down the lane here to make that call. I'm not as young as I was, and no spring chicken anymore and I can tell you I was jiggered when I finally got back home.'

'Yes, I'm sure you were Miss Matthews but thank you for making the call. Please go on.'

'Well, you see it was like this, I was just about to turn in for the evening and as you can imagine, we don't get much traffic down this lane. It's normally people who are lost and in need of directions, it's a dead end you see at the bottom of the lane. I mean there was no way I was going out in the dark to give any directions to anyone at that time of night I can tell you. Anyway, this car pulls up just outside the gate and whoever it was kept the engine running, bloody inconsiderate if you ask me. Actually, it was just about where you've parked. God knows what he or she was doing down here, unless it was two lovers of course looking to have a bit of nooky in a quiet spot. I switched the front room light on and as soon as I did, they drove off back down the lane, quick as a flash. I don't think they had realised that someone actually lives here. As you know Mill House farm is not far from here and when I heard about this terrible murder on the news, I thought I'd better ring you.'

'I'm glad you did Miss Matthews. So can you tell me what colour this car was?

'Ooh no, no it was far too dark to see and my eyes are not too good these days anyway.'

'Right, well you mentioned they, how many people were in the car?'

'Did I? oh yes, well I could only see one, the driver. There may have been others in there for all I know but it was far too dark you see. I don't mind telling you it scared me a bit. I didn't sleep well at all after that, I always keep the doors locked and bolted. I was awake most of that night making tea, I couldn't sleep at all after that.'

'And at one time of night did you see this car?'

'Ooh I couldn't say, I suppose it would be about 11 o'clock, I'm not really sure to be quite honest.'

'And can you remember which night it was?'

'Oh yes, it was Sunday. I'd been listening earlier to "*Your hundred best tunes*" with Alan Keith on the wireless. Yes, it was definitely Sunday night or come to think of it was it Saturday? You've got me thinking now. No, it must have been Sunday evening, of course it was. Are you sure you don't want a cup of tea?'

'No thank you very much Miss Matthews,'

'Well, how about a slice of homemade cake perhaps, it's very tasty?'

'No, I'm fine thank you.'

'That's about it, I can't tell you much more than that really.'

'Well, if there is anything else that you think of please don't hesitate to call the incident room. I'll be off now but thank you for your time Miss Matthews, it's much appreciated,' said DS Bradshaw as he started to make his way to the front door.

'Are you sure you won't just stop for a cup of tea, I don't often have much company these days, it's a bit lonely out this way?'

'No, thank you I'm fine but thanks again for all your help Miss Matthews.'

'Not at all Officer. Oh, hang on, just a minute, yes, there was something, I just remembered when I switched the light on the man was already out of the car. Did I not mention that? I think he may have just been relieving himself against the hedge or something like that. He soon shot off I can tell you although I think he may have had a bit of a limp.'

***

DC Blackwell had been actioned by the DCI to interview Owen Nixon again regarding his phone call about the vehicle sighting. He decided to go over to his cottage which was just a few miles down the lane from the Smiths farmhouse at Saughall.

'Now I've been through your statement Mr Nixon and I am hoping you might be able to provide us with a little more information on that car you spotted when you were driving home. You were just leaving the farm, is that right?'

'Yes, that's right Officer, it had been a hard night working on that lot at Mill House farm. I was driving home and I saw this car parked half on the grass half on the lane. Well, I remembered afterwards, I think there was only one person in it, I couldn't see anyone on the passenger side unless they were crouched down of course.'

'Did you get a look at the driver at all?'

'No, it was much too dark really and in any case he or she had their head stooped down as I drove past.'

'Can you describe the car?'

'No not really, it was an old model, probably grey I think but it was too dark to see really. I did notice as I slowed down it had a towbar. Sorry I can't be of any more help.'

'No problem Mr Nixon. Well, if there is anything else that comes to mind, give us a ring over at Blacon.'

***

Buckley town centre
Friday, 1ˢᵗ December 1967, 18.00

Jonno and Evo had finished their morning shift earlier in the day and they now had a long weekend ahead of them. They had not heard anything from Sid now for a couple of weeks and they had assumed that he must have been ill. He hadn't been seen on the bus going to work and they thought that he may have even started driving to work using his new found wheels. They had decided to walk down to the Lane End working men's club which was one of Sid's regular drinking places.

As they approached the town centre, a large crowd had gathered just near to the cross roads in readiness for the switching on of the 1967 Christmas lights. Some families had been waiting patiently since 4pm and the atmosphere was now growing by the minute. A large group of well-behaved but very excited children supervised presumably by their teachers and parents stood outside the local newsagents waiting in anticipation for the switch on. The local Board primary school had also decided to hold their annual carol service at the nearby Tabernacle Church Hall on the same night and the town was now buzzing with excitement. All the shops were lit up with decorations in every window. A small group of carol singers with lanterns had gathered near the library and were stood on the Buckley baths steps. The carol singers were now just preparing to sing and almost on cue as if it had been ordered to the minute it started to snow. Just a small fleck at first but then flurries soon followed and within minutes the main roads were covered with a blanket of white as the choir opened with their performance of '*Hark the Herald Angels*'.

'I've never seen the town so busy as this, it looks and sounds fantastic, what a great atmosphere,' remarked Evo as they weaved their way through the waiting crowds, 'well apart from the jubilee day processions of course. I mean this is December and the place is heaving with people coming out on such a cold night.'

'Yeah, I agree, still it's good to see the town thriving and do you know it does almost feel like Christmas now. Come on, let's get a move on if we are to have any chance of seeing Sid.'

The snow was starting to stick now and the roads and pavement were becoming white over. Some twenty five minutes later and after an increased walking pace they eventually strolled into the Lane End working men's club. They signed the visitors' book at the table at the entrance and wandered over to the bar to order their first beers of the evening.

'I don't suppose you've seen Sid Longshaw in here recently?' asked Jonno as he handed over a ten-shilling note to the barman.

'Sid, no it's funny you should say that, we were only talking about him the other day. Sid usually comes in here early doors when he has been on the six-till-two shift. We haven't seen him or his dad in here for ooh I'd say it must be a week or two now. We assumed he was ill or something.'

'Well, if you see Sid, can you tell him Jonno and Evo have been asking after him.'

'I will indeed and if you see him first tell him the lads up at the top club would like to see him. He still owes me a bob or two from the last snooker game we had together,' laughed the barman as he handed the change over to Jonno.

Jonno and Evo took their drinks into the adjacent games room, two young lads were just finishing their game on the snooker table. Jonno placed a two-shilling piece on the side of the table and took a seat with Evo in the far corner and waited for the snooker table to become available.

'Do you know it beats me what's happened to him, it's like he's disappeared off the face of the earth,' said Evo as he took the top off his pint and wiped the froth off the top of his mouth, 'I mean it's not like him. I did think about calling round at his house but last time I went his mum told me to clear off, she said I was a bad influence or something like that. I got the impression she doesn't like me much.'

'To be honest I was asking some of his workmates on the bus and they said he hasn't been in work for a good while. He'll turn up like a bad penny, he normally does. Still I miss his company, he's a good laugh is Sid. Come on, the table is free now, let's see if you are as bad as last time. Loser buys the pickled eggs!'

***

Jane Sheraton was busy preparing a lamb hot-pot supper in readiness for when Michael returned home. It was Mike's favourite and she wanted to surprise him. Their daughter Janet, despite her dad's advice and concerns had gone off to the local youth club. Since this latest incident Michael realised it could have been his own daughter in that Saughall fire and they had had a huge row when he had advised her to stay at home and not make the journey down to the local youth club. Michael had phoned home earlier in the day and said he should be home about 6.30pm but as of yet there had been no sign of him. The Sheratons lived in a large old ivy clad detached house on a very nice secluded pre-war estate near Rowton, close enough to the city centre but quiet enough to enjoy the surrounding Cheshire countryside. It was now 7.15pm and there was still no sign of him. Jane however was used to this having been married to him for almost twenty-five years she knew she had to expect him whenever he could get away. She'd lost count of the number of times she'd had to warm up his dinner in the oven or on a plate over a pan of boiling water. Despite this they had a strong marriage but she was now finally looking forward to his retirement. She had hardly seen him all week as he'd naturally been tied up with this latest investigation. She was just drawing the curtains in the front room when his car at last pulled into the driveway. Minutes later Michael arrived through the front door clearly exhausted. Normally he would either whistle or shout to her as he stepped into the hall but tonight there was nothing. He dropped his briefcase in the hallway, hung his overcoat up on the umbrella stand and collapsed in a heap in his usual armchair by the open fire.

'Had a good day love?' said Jane as she poured her husband a glass of his favourite rose wine.

'So, so love, we don't seem to be getting any nearer on identifying the victim in this case. Missing Persons have drawn a blank and up till now we have no means of identifying her. On top of all that old Duckworth is chasing me every half hour for progress.'

'Well, I'm sure someone must be missing her whoever she was. You'll see, something will turn up. Dare I mention in your conversations with him whether you have spoken to ACC Duckworth yet about you finishing?'

'There's no chance of that love, but I will, one day but not yet. Not just yet.'

***

Beaumaris, North Wales
Saturday, 2nd December, 7.30am

Nancy Ellis rose earlier than normal on that Saturday morning. She had hardly had any sleep at all and been up all night worrying why she hadn't heard from her daughter Jenny. She had watched the clock almost every hour, been up making numerous cups of teas and simply couldn't get off to sleep. Nancy had moved from Chester after her first husband Harold had passed away following a long illness. Widowed at the age of just turned forty-one Nancy had been left to bring up their only daughter on her own. She thought the world of her, they were very close. Whenever they were out together Jenny and her mum were always mistaken as sisters, the resemblance was uncanny. Nancy had had no intention or desire of finding anyone after losing her beloved Harold but a chance meeting at an old school reunion evening led to a whirlwind romance and she went on to marrying her old classmate Keith Ellis within eight months. Jennifer hadn't been keen on the relationship but she finally accepted it. Nancy and Keith had settled in Beaumaris where he worked as a marine engineer at a local boatyard. Keith was six months younger than Nancy and he'd always fancied her when they were in secondary school together but they had lost touch after leaving school. He'd been divorced not long after his first marriage, walking out and leaving his wife and a young son.

Keith had failed miserably to support his ex-wife and son and now they were no longer in touch. To Keith it was as if they had never existed.

Nancy went downstairs, made another pot of tea and this time took a tray up to her husband who was still in bed snoring his head off. She placed the china cup and saucer on the bedside table, switched the bedside lamp on and as gently as possible shook Keith out of his slumbers.

'For god's sake what, what is it now woman? Bloody hell Nancy please let me sleep, it's my day off,' said Keith as he turned over, 'Can't you see I've had a hard week on nights. I do need a bit of a lie in this morning. Can't it wait?'

'Keith, it's not like her, I mean she rings me every Friday evening without fail, do you think she's alright, I'm worried sick?'

'Who, not like who? What on earth are you on about this time?' said Keith still rubbing his eyes and trying to prop himself up on the pillows.

'Our Jenny of course, she hasn't rung me. She normally rings me every Friday. Every Friday night without fail even if it's only just for a few minutes to have a quick chat. We'll have to go up there, she could be ill for all we know. Something's happened to her I know it.'

'Perhaps as you say she is probably ill and it's just a bit of a cold or flu symptoms or something like that, there's a lot of it about you know. Stop worrying yourself love, she'll ring you later, you'll see, now just let me get back to sleep, I'm exhausted.'

'Yes, I suppose you're right love, I'll ring her boss on Monday morning, I won't bother the shop at present.'

'I think you are worrying over nothing. Now close the door and let me get back to some shuteye.'

***

Chester city centre
Saturday, 2nd December 1967, 11.30am

The city centre was busier than ever on the Saturday morning with only three weeks before Christmas the shoppers were in town bright and early. The place was bustling and DS Bradshaw decided to park his car in the HQ car park and walk into the city centre. He'd wished he had chosen a weekday to visit the many jewellery shops in the city but he had been faced really with no choice and the DCI had insisted they had to work at least part of the weekend. However, he'd prepared for this task well in advance by drawing up a list of shops that could have possibly sold the Sekonda gold watch and had it engraved. There were six potential shops on his list and Sekonda being a new brand of British watch which was actually made in Russia had only been made available a year earlier in 1966. He felt therefore there was a good chance that it had been bought recently in the area and together with the engraving hopefully someone might just remember it being sold. Deep down he knew it was a long shot but it had to be done if they were to get close to identifying the victim. He had already visited five shops and drawn a blank on each of them. Sure, they had sold Sekonda watches but none of them recognised that particular type which was slightly unusual with its twisted gold-plated strap. They also had no records of any engraving nor kept any records of the actual customer, most choosing to buy the watch with cash. He was beginning to think that he'd had a bit of a wasted journey when he arrived at the tiny shop hidden down a side street from the city centre. He pushed open the door to the sound of a large irritating bell as he entered the doorway. The jewellery shop was tucked away down the bottom of Watergate Street not far from the Infirmary. Jim had to wait a few minutes while the elderly sales assistant completed the purchase of a lady's silver necklace.

'Can I help you sir?' said the assistant as he replaced the tray of jewellery into the glass cabinet.

DS Bradshaw retrieved his warrant card from his inside pocket.

'Yes, DS Bradshaw, Cheshire Police. I gather you are a dealer of Sekonda watches and wondered if you have kept records of watches that you may have engraved.'

'Yes, we are one of the Sekonda dealers in the area, the watches have only been available since last year I believe. How can we be of assistance?'

'Well, would you recognise this particular type of watch?' said the DC removing a photograph from his pocket.

'Yes, I recognise that particular type which is starting to becoming popular. It's quite rare with that type of strap though I must say. It's possible that someone may have had it engraved and it could have been bought here but I'm afraid we don't keep records of the actual wording that we would have been asked to engrave. There's not a lot of calls for watch engraving. In any case the watch could have been engraved elsewhere of course as some people do prefer that option.'

'Yes of course. Tell me will you have a record of the purchasers of these watches?'

'Oh, yes, I can get that for you, we do keep a register. Old Mr Hassall the owner of the shop is a stickler for keeping records, not sure why to be honest but he's always done it, bit of a tradition with him, I think. You are most welcome to see that. Just a minute I'll get it from the back of the shop.'

The little shop was now getting busy with hardly any room to manoeuvre. With only one shop assistant a queue had also now started to form. Minutes later the old man came back with what at first sight looked to be like an old tatty school exercise book.

'There we are, this is the book we would have recorded our watch sales on, it's all in date order and gives you the customer name and the type of watch purchased, as I said I'm afraid we don't keep a record of any engravings. Now if you don't mind Officer, I really must get on with serving these other customers. I'm afraid you can't take the book with you but please feel free to see if you can find what you are looking for.'

DS Bradshaw thanked the assistant and managed to find himself a quiet corner in which to work through the pages. He started to browse through the handwritten ledger which in places was completely illegible. The entries in the book went back decades and the shop had been quite thorough in recording each customer but at least he only needed to go back a year. After about thirty minutes Jim however soon had what he wanted a list of seven potential names. He jotted down the names, handed the exercise book back over to the assistant and decided to follow up the names and dates back at the incident room.

***

Saltney, Flintshire
Monday, 4th December, 9.30am

The grocery shop was always a bit quieter on the Monday mornings and Norman and Joan always used the opportunity to check and restock the grocery shelves after the weekend's rush. Joan had assumed now that not having heard from Jennifer that she must be on holiday and thought she was probably staying at her mother's house on Anglesey. Norman was just armed with his clipboard about to enter the stock room when he received a phone call.

'Bells Grocery Store, can I help you?'

'Oh hello, my name is Nancy Ellis, is that Norman?'

'It is yes, how can I be of help?' replied Norman thinking to himself that it must be one of his regular customers that knew his name but he couldn't somehow recollect the voice or even the name.

'I'm Jennifer's mum, you know, Jennifer who works with you. We haven't met, she often spoke about you but I wonder if I could have a quick chat with her?'

'Oh right, yes of course. Well, I'm afraid she's not here Mrs Ellis, we haven't heard from her to be honest since Saturday. I think she has taken a few days off on holiday. It's strange really as she didn't enter anything into the holiday book and I can only assume she has gone away perhaps.'

Joan who was about to grab a large box of tinned tomatoes from the stock room stopped what she was doing at this point and eavesdropped on the conversation.

'Well, I'm worried as she normally rings me every weekend mostly on a Friday evening without fail but we haven't heard a word from her since the previous week. I thought she would have first contacted you if she was planning to go away. Have you any idea whether she is ill or not?'

'No Mrs Ellis, we haven't heard anything from her.'

Suddenly at this point Joan remembered hearing something on the news about a girl's body that had been found recently and thought to herself, *Surely, it couldn't be her,* and tried desperately to dismiss it from her mind.

Norman could see Joan was eavesdropping on the phone call and thought just for a split second before answering, choosing his words carefully before responding to Jennifer's mother.

'As you say she could be ill, Mrs Ellis. There is a nasty bout of flu going 'round I believe, perhaps she's in bed with that. I tell you what though, just to ease your mind I'll call round there straight away. Why don't you give me a call back in say an hour or two when I've had a chance to pop round there to see if she is alright.'

'Thank you, Norman, I do appreciate it. I have a Doctor's appointment this morning but I will call you later on this afternoon if that's okay?'

'Perfect, we'll speak later, I am sure everything will be fine.'

Norman replaced the receiver, paused for a moment and shook his head for a moment but then he hit on an idea. He told Joan to look after the shop and slipped his coat on and headed off into the busy car park. Being first in the shop in the morning he always managed to park as close as possible to the grocery store.

Ten minutes later he arrived at the block of flats. He walked across to the entrance which was always left unlocked and proceeded to knock on Jennifer's door. He hadn't noticed that the milk bottles had since gone and there was no sign of post being left in the letter box.

He shouted through the letter box a few times but there was no response, nothing. He decided to walk out across the lawn. It had been raining heavily overnight and the ground was soaking. He stepped across the lawn and peered through her lounge window. He couldn't help but notice that the small window was slightly open and he reached out to try and close it but it was just slightly out of his reach. He was about to tap on the window pane just in case anyone was in fact in there when suddenly he was startled when a firm arm grabbed him from behind and at the same time, he heard a woman's voice, 'That's him Officer, that's the man I saw the other day. He drove off quickly but I'd recognise him anywhere.'

'Lost our keys have we sir?' said the voice.

Norman couldn't turn around to see who was holding him in such a tight grip, he was helpless.

'Let me go, you are hurting me, what do you think you are doing?'

'I should ask you the same question sir. I'm DC Johnson from Cheshire Police, and who might you be?'

'Norman Arrowsmith, let go of me, you are hurting my arm!'

'All in good time sir, I think we'll best continue this conversation down at the police station.'

***

Blacon Police Station
Monday, 4th December, 10.30am

DCI Sheraton was reviewing the Saughall case in the incident room. The ACC Crime had also insisted on attending the review in order that he could update first-hand the senior command meeting which was scheduled for later that same afternoon. The DCI sidled over to the flip chart stand at the end of the room, looked briefly at his notes, lit up a cigarette and paused for a brief moment before addressing his team. By now the room was full of smoke, everyone in the incident room smoked and used the opportunity to have a short break from the tasks in front of them.

'A week has now gone by and we still haven't got a definite identification of our victim. All we know at present is she was aged between 18 and 25 probably about 5'3 judging by the size 5 shoe found at the scene and the pathology report we've now received. Someone must know this girl yet no one has come forward to report her missing. It is now clear from the report she was murdered away from the fire and therefore we have not just one location but two possible scenes to deal with. Someone must have seen something suspicious, a vehicle, screams, noises anything out of the ordinary. This was a quiet rural area and apart from the odd tractor or excavator working the fields there would be very few vehicles using those country lanes and particularly that time at night. We will be renewing our appeal later this evening so hopefully someone will come forward.'

'DC Blackwell, what have we found so far on missing persons?'

'Nothing definite I'm afraid sir, we have widened the Misper area to include North Wales and Merseyside Police just in case. To date we have received all of their missing female records and we are gradually working our way through them.'

'Good, keep that going and let me know when you have a short-list of possibles, we may have to make a further appeal to the public on this one.'

The DCI checked his notes again and glanced over to DS Bradshaw who was busy typing up an officer's report in the far corner.

'So, DS Bradshaw, any progress on that shoe that was found at the scene?'

'Nothing on that sir, we only know it was a size 5 and could have been bought from any Marks and Spencers store.'

'So what have we got so far with the engraved watch and charm bracelet, anything at all, do we know where they could have been bought?'

'Ah, well I'm working on that now sir, the charm bracelet was pretty much standard, it could have been bought anywhere and there could be thousands of those in circulation. So I have concentrated rather on the watch and that engraving. From the visit to a number of jewellers in the city centre we have seven potential names of those who have bought that particular type of watch. It's a relatively new make and brand, it's good quality yet affordable.'

'And do any of these names have the initials J or N?'

'Three of them do sir but of course it's possible the watch could have been bought by someone other than J or N as a present perhaps so I'm certainly not discounting those at this stage…'

'Good thinking Bradshaw, keep up the good work,' interjected the ACC who had been sitting stroking his chin quietly in the corner and just observing the meeting.

'Thank you, sir,' continued DS Bradshaw as he nodded over to the ACC, 'erm we are indexing the seven possible ones I've found and trying to obtain their addresses as I speak and we will be contacting them in due cause.'

'Did you not manage to obtain addresses from the jewellers then?' interrupted the ACC once again.

'I'm afraid not sir, just the names of the customers, that was all that was recorded on the ledger. The watches were mainly bought with cash. I should say of course that it is possible that the watch we found by the fire was even bought outside the county and the seven names are from people outside the area, tourists for example.'

'Yes, I'm afraid of that but we must follow it up,' responded the DCI now looking somewhat disappointed, 'now look, reading the statements that we have so far, I'm uneasy at the responses from Mr Albert Smith, his son Kenneth and those three farm workers. At this stage I don't want to even discount their possible involvement in this. I am satisfied with the vet's statement. DC Blackwell, I want you to re-interview them starting with the Smiths themselves. Get them in here and I want to be present at their interviews. Understood?'

'Yes sir, straight away sir.'

'The other thing that we mustn't lose sight of is that the slaughtering of the animals took place mostly on the Saturday and actually finished off on the Sunday evening. It is possible that whoever is responsible for this could have moved the body into the fire on the Sunday prior to it being lit. Although I tend to believe that the body was actually placed in the fire on the Sunday evening after they had lit the fires. Okay chaps, let's get back on with it, we all have a lot to do.'

The DCI and the ACC Crime packed their briefcases and started to leave the incident room to head back in DCI Sheraton's car to Force HQ.

'Do you really think one or more of those five down at the farm could be involved in this Mike?' said the ACC as they made their way down the stairs.

'I think one of them could be involved sir. I'll say this I'm far from happy with Kenneth Smith's statement.'

***

Saltney
Monday, 4th December 1967, 2pm

Nigel Simpson appeared to be quite concerned on why Jennifer hadn't turned up for work on the Saturday evening. She had acted a bit strange that night over a week ago when he last saw her. He'd once again offered to walk her to the taxi rank that night but she wasn't haven't any of it, in fact she appeared to be giving him the cold shoulder. He'd noticed a change in her recently and that she had become somewhat distant with him, almost not wishing to get into any conversation at times. He was trying to think back on whether he had said something to offend her at all. She had never been absent before and even when she had been ill and needed time off, she always called him giving him plenty of notice to find replacement bar staff. Fortunately, this week he had managed to persuade one of his Sunday staff to come in at a last minute's notice. The bars and restaurants were busier than ever this time of year with the various Christmas office parties and he certainly had his hands full organising staff for all three of the nightclub bars. He sat at home pondering on what he should do if anything, it was bothering him. Maybe she would call him at the nightclub later in the week. There was no telephone in the flats so he decided to call round and see if she was ill and if there was anything she needed. He wasn't quite sure where she lived but at least he had her address in his work diary. He drove over to Saltney and parked his car illegally in one of the residents parking spots. He checked the flat number on his notes and made his way through into the foyer. Foyer was too grand a word for it really, just a dank hallway with a concrete floor. There was a strong smell of bleach and some evidence of graffiti still daubed on one wall where someone had failed trying to clean it off. Being on the ground floor it was easy enough to find and he rang the doorbell. He waited for a few more minutes and tried again. Nothing not a sound. In fact, the block of flats seemed totally deserted. He thought maybe she had gone away, he remembered that her mother lived on Anglesey so perhaps she had gone there for a short break but odd that she'd never mentioned having some time off. Soon he was heading back to his flat in the city centre.

***

'Good morning, Bells Grocery store.'

'I'm sorry to bother you but can I speak to Norman please?'

'I'm afraid he is not here at present. I can ask him to ring you when he comes back. Who shall I say is calling?'

'Oh, it's Nancy Ellis, Jennifer's mum. I rang earlier and Norman said he would pop round to see if our Jennifer is ill, we haven't heard from her for over a week now.'

'Oh, yes, hello Mrs Ellis. Norman mentioned to me that you had called and to be quite honest we are not sure where he is now. He was on his way to Jennifer's place and I can't think why he hasn't been back here by now. It shouldn't have taken him more than twenty minutes. We are getting a bit concerned ourselves to be honest, he said he wouldn't be long.'

'I'm really very sorry to have bothered you, as you can tell we are quite worried. It's probably best if we drive across to see her. Please tell Norman that I called when you see him.'

'It's no bother at all Mrs Ellis, I'll certainly tell Norman you have called.'

Nancy replaced the receiver and slumped back into the armchair.

This wasn't at all what Nancy Ellis had wanted to hear, she was clearly hoping that Norman would tell her that all was well and Jennifer was at home safe and sound, maybe just having a few days off. There was nothing for it now but to head over to Saltney.

***

Blacon Police Station
Monday, 4th December 1967, 2.30pm

'I shall ask you once again, Mr Arrowsmith, what exactly were you doing sneaking around that block of flats in Saltney and in particular peering through the front window of one of the flats?'

'I wasn't "sneaking around" as you call it.'

'Okay what would you call it then?'

'I keep telling you, one of my fellow employees Jennifer lives there and she had not turned in for work and I went to see if she was ill or not.'

'So, you took it on yourself to abandon your post in a busy grocery shop to go and see if she was ill or not?'

'Yes, that's right.'

'Do your employers know that you do this sort of thing?'

'Erm, no, erm what do you mean, what sort of thing?'

'So you would do that for all your fellow employees would you? A sort of community service provided on your part, a goodwill gesture if you like, a sort of welfare officer role.'

'Erm no, well yes. Look, I knew where Jennifer lived and her mother had been on the phone to me asking why she hadn't heard from her. We were also worried that something might have happened to her. I said that I would go 'round to her place and see if she was ill or something. Her mother rang me, why don't you ask her?'

'Oh, we will Mr Arrowsmith, we will.'

'Look, why don't you believe me, I'm telling you the truth. I need to get back to work you know, I have a shop to run!'

'Yes, I quite realise that. All in good time Mr Arrowsmith. So when you got there you found the door was locked and you decided to creep around the building. You then decided to try one of the small windows presumably to gain access to the flat?'

'No, no it wasn't like that. I wasn't creeping as you put it. Look, I couldn't help noticing that the small window was slightly open and I was just trying to reach out to close it just in case of any burglars in the area.'

'A likely story. Do you really expect me to believe that Mr Arrowsmith?'

'Well, it's the truth I tell you.'

'We will of course check your story Mr Arrowsmith but how do you account for the bag of tools that we found in the back of your car,' replied DC Johnson as he looked down at his notepad, 'namely a rope, hessian sacking, sledgehammer and a crowbar. Don't tell me these are the tools of your trade that are required in your grocery shop?'

'Look, I've been working on my mother's old house, taking down an old conservatory over the last weekend. I've left them in the boot of the car, it's not a crime is it?'

'And the blood-stained rags we also found in the boot?'

'Erm, I cut myself on some glass in the process of dismantling the conservatory.'

'Another likely story Mr Arrowsmith, to be honest I'm surprised we didn't find a mask and a striped tee shirt in the bag at the same time.'

'I'm telling you the truth I tell you. Now can I please go, I need to get back to work before my boss finds out that I'm missing.'

'All in good time Mr Arrowsmith, all in good time.'

***

Cheshire Police HQ
Tuesday, 5th December 1967, 9am

'Good morning, Missing Persons section, WPC Curson speaking how can I be of help?'

'Oh, good morning, my name is Nancy Ellis, I've been put through by your headquarters switchboard. I'm worried about my daughter Jennifer who seems to have gone missing. I've been over to her flat and there is no sign of her. I'm worried sick, is there anything you can do…'

'Firstly, let me put your mind at ease Mrs Ellis. Any reports of missing people are taken very seriously by the force and we will devote considerable time and resources to finding them wherever we can. It could be of course that your daughter has gone away and maybe somehow forgotten to let you know.'

'She would have told me she was going away. I know she would, I'm sure something is wrong.'

'Well, our priority now is to share the information across the region Mrs Ellis and always try to locate the missing person and make sure they are at least safe and well.'

'Oh, I do hope so, I've been going out of mind worrying about her.'

'I'm sure you have Mrs Ellis so let me take down some details. Firstly, what was your daughter's full name?'

'Jennifer Linda Webb.'

'I thought you said your name was Ellis madam?'

'Yes, I've remarried my daughter is Jennifer Webb.'

'Ah right, sorry about that and when did you last hear from your daughter Mrs Ellis?'

'I suppose it was just over a week ago now. She normally calls me every Friday evening without fail for a chat but she didn't ring last Friday and I'm now getting concerned. I've also been in touch with her workplace and just visited her flat which looks as though it hasn't been occupied for quite a few days. Her neighbour says she has also been in touch with the Police to report her missing. It's not like Jennifer to go off like this without telling anyone.'

'Right Mrs Ellis, we just need some more details from you and we will also need from you a recent photograph but if you hear from her in the meantime please let us know immediately. Let's hope she is safe and well.'

WPC Curson continued to take further details from Nancy Ellis and filled out the appropriate paperwork which would eventually be typed up and filed accordingly however she wasted no time in calling the Blacon incident room.

***

Blacon Police Station, Incident Room
Tuesday, 5th December 1967, 9.30am

'Is that Detective Constable Johnson?'

'No madam, this is DS Bradshaw, how can I help you?'

'Oh, my name is Edith Flowers, can you please pass a message onto him?'

'Yes of course madam.'

'Well, he was over here yesterday and I wish to report another strange man in a grey Austin car has been visiting my neighbour's flat and what's more he parked it in my parking spot.'

'Did you manage to get the vehicle registration madam?'

'Yes, I did it was VUX42, I wrote it down.'

'Thank you, madam, I'll pass it straight onto DC Johnson.'

'Thank you for calling.'

DS Bradshaw scribbled the note and left it on DC Johnson's desk.

***

Blacon Police Station, Interview Room 2
Tuesday, 5th December 1967, 11.00am

Albert Smith sat uneasily in the chair, he'd not been happy that he'd been called away from the farm and his body language in the interview room certainly showed it. He'd been working in the empty fields repairing a few broken fences when Kenneth came to him saying he'd received a request asking for him to attend the police station as soon as possible. Albert had managed to get a quick wash, changed out of his boiler suit and driven over to the police station. DC Blackwell tried his best to put the old man at ease and led with the initial questioning.

'Thank you for coming into the station Mr Smith, so can you please repeat for myself and DCI Sheraton your movements on both Saturday 25th and Sunday 26th November.'

'I hope this won't take long. I've work to be getting on with back at the farm you know. I haven't got anything really to add to my original statement.'

'This shouldn't take too long Mr Smith, if you can tell us in your own words what exactly happened after you returned to the farmhouse from the barn on the Saturday evening.'

'Well, it's like I told your other officers earlier, I wasn't there all evening, I couldn't face it see so I returned to the farmhouse and left them to it. We decided to light the fires on the Sunday night once all the slaughtering was complete. On the Sunday I left it all to them, I didn't go near the barn and our Kenneth supervised it all. I just couldn't cope with it all you see, it was heart-breaking seeing those animals destroyed like that.'

'I'm sure it was Mr Smith. So who exactly were you with in the barn before you decided to return to the farmhouse?' asked the DCI who was now leaving DC Blackwell to write the notes at this point.

'Let's see now, there was Bill Lyons the Vet, the two Nixon brothers, their mate Graham and my son Kenneth.'

'I gather one of your regular farmworkers wasn't available that weekend, who was that?'

'Yes, that was James Adams, strange that he'd never had a day off in his life. He's back at work now of course although there is not much for him to do these days.'

'What was the reason he gave you for being off work that weekend?'

'Well, at first he said he had a few things to see to but then told me he wasn't feeling up to coming in. He had a dodgy stomach or so he said. Bit of an odd character is James, good worker though but he does act a bit strange at times.'

'How do you mean, strange?'

'It's like this, he goes into his shell whenever there is a woman on the scene. He's never been married of course and neither is he likely to at his age now. Strong as an ox though, a good worker no less, been with me on the farm for almost twenty years now. We certainly could have done with him whilst we dealt with the livestock and this awful disease, I can tell you.'

'Yes, I'm sure. So tell me Mr Smith how well do you know the other workers who helped you that weekend.'

'Oh, I've known the Nixon boys a long time, strong workers, very reliable. They move from farm to farm wherever there is a job that needs doing. That's how they like it, I suppose it gives them a bit of variety working at different farms and it means we can keep our costs down not having to employ them full time.'

'And their mate Graham?'

'Well, I've never met him before, he seems a nice sort of a lad, certainly helped us out that weekend I can tell you. Likes his beer though, he couldn't wait to get back for a pint or two so he said.'

'Did you make your own way back to the farmhouse from the barn on that Saturday night?'

'Yes of course, I'm not helpless you know.'

'Quite, and at what time was this approximately?'

'Let's see. I guess it would be about eight thirty I suppose, the lads were still working in the barns. They were still piling up the carcasses at the end of the barn when I left them.'

'And at what time did the others come back after the slaughtering on the Saturday?'

'Bill Lyons was the first to come back at about nine thirty, his job was done you see. He called in at the farmhouse to see if I was alright and we had a brew together. We had a good chat about old times Bill and myself. He would have gone from the farm I'd say about ten thirty. Nice chap Bill, I knew his father who used to be our vet years ago.'

'And what time did the others come back from the fields?'

'Well, that would be about eleven o'clock I guess, once they had finished there was nothing more for them to do. The Nixons and their mate Graham went straight off home separately, I think. Kenneth and me had a nightcap together, he had a couple of whiskies and I had a brandy. Large ones of course, I can tell you I needed a stiff drink after all that.'

'And then what?'

'I went up to bed about eleven thirty and left our Kenneth sitting in the front room listening to the wireless.'

'Can I just ask you what happened on the Sunday?'

'Well, we met again at about the same time Sunday evening. There was not much to do as most of the animals had been destroyed the previous evening. I couldn't face any of it again so I stayed at home. The lads were mostly moving the carcasses onto the fires, they then lit them and when finished went home for the night.'

'Can I just return to the Saturday night. So when you finally went to bed, did you get up at all in the night?'

'Aye of course I did, I'm an old man you know, it's very rare that I can sleep straight through these days. I always have to make a trip or two down to the toilet downstairs at my age particularly if I've had a late drink.'

'And had Kenneth gone to bed when you came downstairs to go to the toilet?'

'Erm no, funny you should say that, I thought at first he had gone to bed you see. He had gone from the front room so I assumed he was now in bed but then as I was about to switch the kitchen lights off, I noticed that his keys were missing and the car had gone out of the yard. I presume he'd gone out for petrol or cigarettes or something like that.'

Suddenly Albert Smith realised he had dropped Kenneth in it.

'Ere you are not suggesting he'd had anything to do with this are you?'

'Not at all Mr Smith, we are not suggesting anything at this stage.'

***

Norman Arrowsmith arrived back home completely exhausted just after seven o'clock that night. He'd spent nearly six hours being interviewed at Blacon Police station and had only been allowed to return home pending further investigations. The grocery shop had been closed at six and he was sure his assistant Joan would have locked up on his behalf although they must have been wondering in the shop where on earth he'd got to. He was angry, very angry indeed, he could kick himself for being so stupid. What did he possibly hope to achieve by going over there? He poured himself a stiff drink and sat back in his armchair. He was embarrassed, angry, felt they had humiliated him down at the police station and he now sat there in the darkness in silence, he was drained. But then he hit on an idea.

***

Blacon Police Station, Interview Room 1
Wednesday, 6th December 1967, 09.30am

DCI Sheraton wasted no time in getting Kenneth Smith into the Police station for an interview; in fact, he'd gone around there personally with DS Oldbury to ask him to come down to the station straight away. At first Kenneth Smith was reluctant to come back with them to Blacon making some poor excuse that he had the barns to tidy up, in the end he drove down to the station closely accompanied by DS Oldbury.

As the three of them sat down DS Oldbury offered Ken Smith a coffee and a cigarette which he declined.

DCI Sheraton took a large swig of coffee and hesitated for a moment before opening with his first question.

'So Kenneth, let me get this straight according to your statement after the slaughtering on the Saturday night you went back to the farmhouse and had a nightcap with your father.'

'Yes, that's right.'

'And then you went straight to bed?'

'Yes, that's right.'

'Went to bed straight away, straight after a drink with your father.'

'Yes.'

'No that's not quite correct is it. We understand you left the farmhouse and drove off somewhere.'

Suddenly Kenneth Smith went bright red, shifted in his seat and started to get very defensive.

'No comment.'

The DCI was a master at using the silence to build up the tension in the interview room and paused for what seemed like hours before continuing.

'Well Kenneth, did you or did you not leave the farmhouse after having a drink with your father on the Saturday night?'

'No comment.'

'Now come on Kenneth, we know you left the farm. Your father said the car had gone and you were the only two people there. So did you leave the farmhouse after having a drink with your father?'

Kenneth Smith looked down and then sighed reluctantly.

'Erm yes, yes, I went to see my girlfriend over in Saltney.'

'So why on earth did you tell us differently.'

'Because I thought I'd get into trouble as my car insurance had run out. With all the worry and all the foot and mouth problems I'd completely forgotten to renew it. I've paid it now, I just thought you lot would be onto me.'

'We have bigger fish to fry than that I can assure you,' responded the DCI, 'so your girlfriend can verify that you were at her address?'

'Yes, she can.'

'And her name?'

'Why you don't really need to speak with her surely?'

For a minute, DS Oldbury thought he'd misheard Ken Smith and was about to write down the name Shirley.

'If we are to believe your story, yes, we do. So what's her name?'

'Her name is Sheila Gilderson.'

'And her address?'

Kenneth Smith hesitated for a brief moment.

'17 Famau view, I was with her, she'll vouch for me, just ask her.'

'Oh, we will Kenneth, we will.'

***

Saltney
Wednesday, 6th December 1967, 11.30am

DC Blackwell had dropped everything and been given the priority action to go and interview Kenneth Smith's girlfriend to corroborate his movements on that Saturday night. The house was easy to find just off the main Saltney Chester road. He parked his car at the end of the avenue and soon found number 17 which looked out of place with the rest of the surrounding properties. The house badly needed some urgent care and attention. The garden was overgrown with weeds and the windows and doors badly needed repainting. One of the small front room windows had been smashed and had been roughly repaired using some sort of hardboard or plywood. As he rang the doorbell, he could hear someone moving around inside and as he stood back a few paces just managed to catch a glimpse of someone moving around in an upstairs bedroom window. He waited for a few minutes but it was silent, not a sound. He rang the doorbell again and this time he heard footsteps on the stairs and seconds later a young red-haired lady who looked to be no more than eighteen years came to the door, chewing gum, wearing just a white dressing gown and a pair of pink fluffy slippers.

'Erm, good morning Miss,' said the DC showing his warrant card, 'I'm looking for Miss Sheila Gilderson?'

'Yes, that's me Officer,' she replied as she continued to chew gum and looked quite shocked.

'There's nothing to worry about miss but can I come in, I just need to ask you a few questions, it won't take me a minute?'

'I haven't time, it's not really convenient at the moment Officer.'

'Well, it won't take a minute, I assure you, we just need to clarify something with you.'

At that moment a man's voice could be heard shouting down from upstairs.

'Who is it love, what do they want?'

'I'll be back up in a minute, keep your bleeding hair on,' replied Sheila Gilderson as she shouted back up the stairs.

'Look it really isn't convenient at present Officer.'

'Well, okay miss, can you just confirm that you are the girlfriend of a Kenneth Smith from Mill House farm, Saughall?'

'Girlfriend is putting it a bit strong I suppose but yes, I know Kenneth, why? Has he done something wrong that I should know about?'

'No miss, well not that we know of but can you confirm that you met with him late on Saturday night, 25th November?'

'Well, I'll have to have a look at my diary but yes, it's quite possible, I do tend to see him late at night on the odd occasion.'

'Who is it love, get rid of whoever it is.' came the angry voice again from the top of the stairs.

'Look, can't it wait Officer, I am a bit busy at present.'

'Alright miss, look I can see it's clearly inconvenient at present but we may need you to make a statement. I'll be in touch. Thanks for your help.'

DC Blackwell decided he'd wasted enough time standing on the doorstep and made his way back to the car but before he did, he just happened to look back at the upstairs window and was surprised to see not one but three faces in the bedroom window.

***

Blacon Incident Room
Friday, 8th December 1967, 11.00am

DS Bradshaw was busy reviewing the outstanding actions with the major incident team from the week in readiness for the SIO's afternoon meeting.

'So how did you get on with that girlfriend of Kenneth Smith, what was her name again?

'Sheila Gilderson, sir,' replied DC Blackwell as he continued to file his paperwork.

'Aye, that's right, so could she corroborate his statement?'

'Well, not exactly Sarge, I don't think it's his girlfriend.'

'What do you mean, it's not his girlfriend? He was quite specific, he'd been with her late at night.'

'To put it bluntly, I think he's been visiting a knocking shop.'

'And you went to visit her?' replied the DS who looked completely shocked.

The entire office suddenly fell about laughing but stopped abruptly when the DI entered the office unannounced.

'I can see you lot are having a good time here. Haven't you got anywhere with those mispers yet John?' asked DI Smethurst impatiently, 'The boss will be here in a minute and he's expecting an update on all of this.'

'To be honest boss with taking on some of the other actions it's taken me most of the time indexing the additional ones we've now received from the other forces. I haven't had time to check each one first. There are a couple of possibles that I have spotted for example with the right age group etc and I've added them onto the category card for *Possible Missing Persons.*'

'What! Look forget the damn manual indexing for now, let's look through the actual forms you've received from the other forces. It's imperative that we try and identify this poor girl as soon as possible and we start from a local perspective as a priority not outside the bloody force area.'

DC Johnson sat listening to this across the desk from DC Blackwell and he wasn't sure whether he should interrupt the DI who was in one of his foul moods again, in the end he thought he'd better say something.

'I'm sorry to butt in boss but we've now had two separate local reports of the same person missing – Jennifer Webb who hasn't been seen for over ten days. I was round at her place the other day following up the first report from her neighbour when I brought in that weird bloke for snooping at her flat. Apparently, her mum has also now reported her missing, she was on the phone the other day.'

The DI looked as though he was going to blow a gasket.

'Right, well make sure we have full details of this girl Jennifer Webb, get hold of her photograph, boyfriend details, etc., etc., and find out who her dentist was, we will need dental records for ID on this one as soon as possible. Pronto understood!'

'Yes sir.'

***

Loggerheads Car Park, Flintshire
Friday, 8th December 1967, 7pm

PC Gwyn Jones and PC Arwel Thomas were in their patrol car and were sat in a layby just outside Mold when they received the radio message asking them to attend the parking area at the Loggerheads Country Park. It had been an unusually quiet night up until now, it would be a while before the pubs called last orders and that's when it could get quite hectic. A suspicious car had been sighted there overnight and had in fact been parked there over several days but it was now the presence of a young man lighting a small fire nearby that had prompted one or two of the local residents to call the Police. The beautiful Loggerheads Country Park follows the course of the River Alyn through karstic limestone countryside and includes the sites of old lead mines and mills. In the summer families would often meet there for picnics and walks through the easily accessible pathways. In the winter however whilst still popular for walks the car park would normally be empty overnight and the locals found it odd they could see a car parked there. At first it looked as though the car had been dumped there as it certainly looked to need some attention.

'It's probably just a couple of lovers Gwyn; in fact I'll let you into a secret: I've thought about using this place myself except the missus would find out!' joked PC Thomas as they parked the car out of sight at the end of the car park, 'Still we'll take a quick look.'

'Well, we used to rely on the car heater instead of lighting a fire,' laughed PC Jones.

'You were lucky to have a car heater, we used to have a picnic blanket!'

It was dark as the two police officers approached the other end of the car park. With no street lighting they edged their way quietly towards the car by torchlight and could see in the distance the glow of a small fire just about ten yards from the abandoned car. As they approached, they could see a young man sitting on a tree stump with his back to them leaning over what looked like a small cooking pot which was finely balanced on top of the open fire.

'Is there enough in there for the two of us as well?' grinned PC Thomas as they got a bit nearer to him.

The young man jumped up, swung around quickly and almost knocked over the pan of baked beans he'd been warming up on the fire, he hadn't heard the two officers and for one split second, he even thought about running off into the woods.

'Erm, no, you frightened me, I didn't see you coming.'

It was then that the two police officers could see the young man was dishevelled, badly dressed and by the smell hadn't clearly washed for a number of days.

'Don't you know that this is a fire hazard, you should have more sense. You really must not light fires in this country park. Can't you see the signs around here. Imagine the damage you could do if that got out of hand.'

'Yes, your quite right, I'm sorry Officer, I hadn't realised. I was hungry you see and needed some warm food inside me. I haven't eaten for a couple of days.'

'You are not planning to sleep here overnight as well are you?' enquired PC Jones.

'Erm, well, yes, I was. I don't have anywhere else to live I'm afraid.'

PC Thomas shook his head and took out his notebook and jotted down the car registration.

'Okay, so what's your full name?'

'Sid Longshaw.'

'And you say you have no fixed address?'

'Well, I did have in Buckley until a couple of weeks back but my stepmother has kicked me out. I've not got anywhere else to go. I've just been staying in this car park since then and going off to work from here.'

'So where exactly do you work then Sid?'

'I used to work at the Shotton steelworks but I'm afraid I've been sacked as I couldn't get there on one or two days, I had no money for petrol you see. Since then I've been getting whatever work I can at farms, odd jobs and the like.'

'So, have you got any petrol now in your car?'

'Yes, I managed to scrape together five shillings and buy myself a gallon of petrol the other day which will tide me over till I can get myself sorted.'

'Well, I tell you what we will do Sid, we clearly have to report that we have attended the incident as some of the locals around here had reported seeing the car. As soon as you have eaten, extinguish that fire straight away and move away from here, understood?'

'Yes, of course, I'm sorry you've been called.'

'That's okay, it's our job, now you should be able to find somewhere like a layby near Mold or Ruthin to park up in for the night. Here's a quid, you are clearly down on your luck lad at present so let's hope things start changing for you real soon.'

'Thank you, Officer, I really appreciate that. I'll be off as soon as I've eaten this.'

The two police officers returned to their vehicle but they couldn't help discussing the poor lad.

'That was kind of you Arwel, giving him a bit of money like that.'

'Well, poor kid, I felt sorry for him having to live like this in the cold. Christmas coming and all that, it could happen to anyone.'

Chapter 10

River Dee, Chester
Sunday, 10th December 1967, 8.00am

Miss Agnes Middleton had recently retired from her lifelong teaching career and just a few months ago had moved from her large old five bedroomed detached house in Handbridge to a brand-new luxury two-bedroomed retirement apartment just down the road overlooking the river Dee in the Lower Park Road. Agnes had taught in a number of the local primary schools in the Chester area and after forty years of dedicated service she had finally decided to call it a day a few months back. Her home had certainly got too big for her, in fact it always had been apart from the times when she had friends coming over to stay for the weekends. On this particular Sunday morning she set off as usual to walk her west highland white dog "Snowy" and to pick up the newspapers en-route. It was a beautifully crisp wintry morning with not a cloud in the sky. Every Sunday morning Agnes always took the same route, walking past the same large impressive Victorian houses and then following the path down across to the suspension footbridge. She told her friends it was all part of her fitness regime and her desire to lose weight which at over twenty stone was proving however very difficult. The

Queen's Park Suspension Bridge connects The Groves on the north side across the river with the affluent Queen's Park area of Chester to the south. Whilst it was bright it was still deceiving and a bitterly cold morning. The riverbank was relatively quiet apart from the occasional jogger, cyclist and dog walker. She shuddered as she witnessed a lone rower on the river heading away from the weir. The city was just waking and as she walked alongside one of the riverside moorings her dog started to bark incessantly just outside the remains of an old decaying boathouse. The dog would simply not move and was rooted firmly to the ground. Try as she might Agnes could not coax the dog to continue with the walk and she could not understand at first what had caused his unusual behaviour. The dog continued to yap and began straining on the lead in the direction of the old boathouse wooden door. She decided to get closer and see what all the fuss was about and then noticed the door to the boathouse was unlocked and had been left slightly ajar. As she got a little nearer, she then caught a smell most foul, a putrid, powerful disgusting smell like rotting garbage or meat that had gone off. She prised open the wooden door and it was then she saw a naked body lying face down on the boatshed floor with a rough hessian sack covering its head. She nearly vomited at the smell and the sight in front of her. She quickly closed the door and paused for a minute to take in large gulps of fresh air. She had to think quickly, there was no one else around on this side of the river, it was still early. With no phone box in sight she walked as quickly as she could past the band stand. She was breathless when she eventually reached the phone box on Lower Bridge Street and frantically dialled 999.

***

Michael Sheraton was just clearing the breakfast dishes from the table before the family were due to head off for a special pre-Christmas church service when the phone rang in the hallway.

'I'll get it!' he shouted as he made his way down the corridor towards the outer hallway, 'It's probably for Janet anyway.'

'If that's Edna, tell her I haven't forgotten her and we will pick her up on the way to church. I'd been meaning to call her, tell her I'm sorry,' shouted Jane from upstairs.

'Will do love,' replied Michael as he picked up the receiver.

'Hello, Michael Sheraton.'

'I'm sorry to trouble you sir on your day off, it's DS Hinckley at HQ I'm afraid we've had another one, this time it's in Chester!'

Michael Sheraton could not believe his ears. They were still struggling with the investigation at Blacon and then this one and just days before Christmas. His first thought however was his family, *Well, unless a miracle shows up now, there goes my Christmas break.*

'Whereabouts?'

'Down by the River Dee sir, down by the Groves in fact in one of the old disused boathouses. Forensics are there already and the pathologist has already been called out.'

'I know the place, right I'll be over there straight away, meet me there.'

He finished the call and bounded up the stairs to pick up his suit jacket which he'd left on top of the bed.

Jane was just getting her coat on in front of the mirror as he entered the bedroom.

'I'm so sorry love you won't believe this but I've been called out to another incident, I will need the car and I'll have to give church a miss this morning. Please make my apologies to everyone. Sorry about this but I will ring you later on when I know what's actually happening.'

***

The DCI wasted no time in getting over to the River Dee, he parked his car as close as he could get to the riverbank and already, he could see a group of spectators including a couple of children who were gathering not far from the bandstand and trying desperately to see what was happening. Two uniformed officers were stood close by attempting to hold them back whilst DS Hinckley stood outside the old boathouse doorway waiting for the DCI's arrival.

'Good morning sir, I'm sorry to have disturbed you this morning.' said the DS immediately he'd seen the DCI arriving.

'Not a problem Derek, let's get on with it shall we and see what we are dealing with here.'

'It's not a pretty sight I'm afraid sir, she's over here.'

'They never are Derek, they never are.'

'Right, get rid of that lot quick and bloody well cordon this entire area off. I don't want anyone who is not involved anywhere near here, understood!' shouted the DCI to the two uniformed officers as he walked across to the boatshed.

'Yes sir,' came the reply in unison.

As soon as he had uttered the words a shout echoed from someone in the gathering crowd. 'Good morning Detective Chief Inspector, is this one connected with that incident over at Saughall?'

The DCI stopped momentarily looked across and he couldn't see at first where the voice had come from and then he half recognised the man from the local press.

'So Officer, is it connected?' repeated the man who was now rudely edging his way to the front of the crowd.

He was a scruffy unshaven individual wearing a shabby khaki mac, horn rimmed spectacles and a lob sided pork pie hat. What looked to be like an old-fashioned camera that wouldn't look amiss in a Victorian museum was strapped over his right shoulder. Sheraton didn't even respond to him, shook his head and thought to himself, *How come the press have got wind on this one already?*

'And get rid of him!' he whispered to one of the officers, 'The sods will be arriving by boat soon if we are not careful, we might even have to cordon off the bloody river!'

As the DCI entered the boatshed the foul smell hit him full on and he quickly placed his handkerchief over his mouth. The pathologist Dr Alan Scott had already arrived together with the scenes of crime officer who was already busy lifting prints from a nearby workbench close to where the body lay. The young girl had now been turned on her back and was now completely covered with a large forensic sheet.

'Okay so what have we got this time Alan?'

'Morning Mike, it's not good I'm afraid,' as he turned over the sheet exposing the badly bruised girls face, 'I'd say a girl of no more than about 20 years of age, significant bruising and strangulation with some kind of twine which has cut deep into her throat. She's been dead I would think for over several days but possibly dumped here recently and I'm a bit surprised no one had noticed this earlier as the surrounding area is normally quite busy. From what I can gather the boatshed door had been left slightly ajar and the smell would have certainly alerted any passer-by. She's been a fighter though I'll say that judging by the massive amount of bruising on her arms and legs she certainly put up quite a struggle.'

'Completely naked?'

'Yes, afraid so Mike, she's been left here naked apart from this hessian sacking which had been placed over her head, oh and a high heeled shoe which we found here placed by her side!'

The DCI was ashen faced, he suddenly realised at this point he had a potential serial killer on the loose.

He hesitated at first and couldn't quite take it all in.

'And there is something else sir, we found this can of petrol close by. On it's side in fact, looks like someone hadn't quite finished here and was disturbed.'

'So, erm who was it exactly who discovered the body Derek?'

'Erm,' looking at his note book, 'a Miss Agnes Middleton sir, she was very upset, she was out walking her dog when she discovered it. One of our officers has taken her into HQ for a strong cup of tea.'

'I'm sure she was. Right, well, I'll get over there and have a chat with Miss Middleton. Let me have your report as soon as you can.'

'You stay here, I'll catch you later in the incident room Derek.'

***

Liverpool Daily Post
Monday, 11th December 1967

Cheshire Murder Squad detectives have begun another major investigation after a women's body was found yesterday in a disused boathouse near to The Groves in Chester.

The horrific discovery was made on Sunday morning by a passer-by and police have now sealed off the entire riverside from the Queen Park suspension bridge down towards Lower Bridge street.

Officers have been scouring the area for evidence and an incident room has been setup at the force HQ. Anyone with information please contact the incident room at Police HQ.

A post mortem examination is yet to take place

***

Cheshire Police Press Briefing
Monday, 11th December 1967, 11.00am

'Arnold Millington, Chester Courier. So with this latest incident yesterday Officer, can we assume there is a serial murderer in our midst?'

DCI Sheraton looked across at the ACC Crime and indicated to him that he would take the question from the floor.

'No Mr Millington, we are not saying that at all. In fact, at this point in time we have no reason to connect the two murders and we will operate a completely separate incident room to handle this investigation.'

'So are you any nearer in identifying the first body found in the Lodge lane field fire?'

DCI Sheraton hesitated for a moment before responding and then chose his words very carefully.

'Well, we believe we are close to identifying the female who was found at Saughall on the morning of the 27th November. Unfortunately, I can't tell you anything more than that at this stage of our investigation.'

The ACC looked surprised at this announcement and tried somewhat to hide his body language but Michael Sheraton saw him from the corner of his eye and knew that as soon as this press review was over he would be called in rapidly to the ACC's office to explain how close they really were on the identification of the Saughall body.

At this point the dishevelled bald-headed reporter immediately stood up to address the rest of the press audience and it was then that the DCI remembered where he had seen him before. It was the man in the pork pie hat down at the riverbank close to the scene of the second incident which he had attended on that first morning.

'Can you therefore please confirm that Cheshire Police have allocated sufficient resources to the investigation of this second incident? I mean as I understand it and according to my sources that you have your work already cut out at Blacon with the first incident and that you are already understaffed.'

The man sat down, looked around, nodded to one of the other reporters and seemed to be pleased with himself. It was then the DCI could hear a few other journalists muttering amongst themselves. The DCI was about to respond but ACC Duckworth was quick to interject.

'That is complete rubbish, I don't know who your so-called sources are but they are completely wrong and that is just a rumour. I can assure you we have a full-strength team at Blacon and we are certainly not understaffed. This second investigation will also have the benefit of a fully resourced investigation team and will be based here at the incident room in Police HQ.'

The muttering had stopped momentarily as a young man towards the back stood up, coughed slightly and nervously raised his hand.

The ACC signalled for him to speak up.

'Erm Jim Edworthy from the Wirral Gazette. So, from this so-called full-strength team that you mention who will be the senior officer leading this latest investigation?'

'That will also be DCI Sheraton who I have every confidence in. Now if there are no further questions that will be all for now.'

The gathering of the press then continued to mutter amongst themselves as they edged the way slowly towards the doorway.

The DCI and ACC waited for the last of the press to finally make their way out of the conference room and then packed up their folders before rising from the table.

'Mike, I think we need a chat as soon as we get back to the office and pronto,' whispered the ACC as he gathered his folder and headed for the door.

***

Cheshire Police HQ
Monday, 13th December 1967, 12.15pm

The ACC waited patiently until the door of his office had been closed firmly shut and that DCI Sheraton had pulled up a chair nearer to the edge of the desk. The DCI waited with baited breath, he knew exactly what was about to come.

The ACC didn't look up at first and continued to write a few more lines on the document that he had been working on. Eventually he put down his pen, removed his glasses, lit up one of his cigarettes and sat back in the chair.

'So then, Mike I'm keen to know how close we are apparently on identifying the Saughall body. This is really good news but firstly why wasn't I told about this before this latest press conference and secondly what actual progress has been made?'

Mike Sheraton now looked somewhat uneasy and shifted forward slightly in the chair.

'Erm yes, sir. Well, I might have been just a little premature on that. I was…'

'PREMATURE, bloody hell Mike if it's not true why on earth did you say it?'

'Well, it's partly true sir and…'

'PARTLY! So are we close to identifying her or not?'

'We have a possible misper, sir, which we haven't fully followed through yet. We are in the process of finding her dental records at this stage. It could be her, to be honest we don't know for certainty. We should know once we have traced her dental records.'

'Bloody hell Mike, COULD BE! You are sailing a bit close to the wind on this one, the press are champing at the bit now expecting some sort of an announcement from us any day soon. They will be like flies round a sodding honeypot now. Let's hope for your sake you get her identified quickly.'

'Yes, I realise that sir, I'm very sorry sir.'

'Well, the damage is done, let's hope we get some news soon. Well, that will be all for now, keep me informed as soon as you have anything on either murder investigation.'

'Yes sir.'

DCI Sheraton returned to his office and sank into the chair, he felt terrible, he had realised his big mistake but was so keen to show that his team had at least made some progress. He reached in the top drawer for his cigarettes and lit up. He'd promised Jane he would give up smoking but at times like this he desperately needed one. He picked up the case folder in front of him, sat back in the chair and suddenly had a thought,

How on earth did the press know the actual field in Saughall?

Chapter 11

Tuesday, 12th *December 1967, 09.30am*

DCI Sheraton sat in his office preparing for the HQ incident team briefing. As the SIO of now two major incidents he had very little time to even think about the plans for the family Christmas get together. They had originally planned to go away to Jane's parents on the south coast near Torquay but she had now already started to make arrangements for them to stay at home. His priority now however was to try and identify the Saughall victim as soon as possible. He wasted no time in calling DC Blackwell at the Blacon incident room.

'Good Morning John, are we any nearer in following up those dental records of that missing girl – Jennifer Webb yet?' asked the DCI impatiently, 'I've got the ACC chasing my arse every hour at present.'

'We should be getting the results anytime soon sir,' replied DC Blackwell, 'it has taken me several phone calls to a number of dentists in North Wales and Cheshire to track down her last known dental practice. At first, we thought that she would have been a patient with a local dentist near where she lived but it appears she had remained with a dentist near Buckley where she grew up apparently. I've now managed to get her latest dental records, she was a regular patient at that practice and we are currently awaiting the report from the odontologist to see if they do actually match our body found in the fire at Saughall. We should hear any day now sir.'

'Good work John, keep me posted, I'll be in HQ all day if you have any news.'

'Will do sir.'

The DCI replaced the receiver, pulled his notes together and hurried across the corridor to the HQ incident room to see how the River Dee incident was progressing and to update the incident team on the direction of enquiry. As he entered the incident room, he couldn't help noticing how lively this one was compared with Blacon. In the corner he couldn't help but notice one of the newly assigned uniformed officers to the incident who was holding court with a number of other officers. A tall, jolly, slightly overweight man with a receding hairline and a large bushy moustache who looked vaguely familiar. He was busy just finishing the punchline of a joke to the delight of his fellow officers gathered around him. The DCI caught his eye, then remembered who he was, it was a PC he hadn't seen for some years in fact he'd been on a training course with him at Hendon Police college. They had shared a few drunken nights down there based at the college. The DCI hoped deep down that the officer would not relay any of their shared past in the incident room, after all he had a reputation to defend.

'It's Martin Walker isn't it?' said DCI Sheriton as he approached him, 'Good god, I haven't seen you since we were both PCs together on that course down London. How are you, where've you been, I thought you must have retired by now?'

'Mike, I heard it was you as the SIO on this case, oh sorry I mean sir, yes, it's good to see you after all these years, you've done well for yourself. Here you are as a DCI and me, well I'm just happy still being a PC, never managed to pass the old sergeant's examination and been based down at Congleton for the past fifteen years. It's good to see you again.'

'Yes, likewise Martin, good to have you on the team, welcome on board and talking about the team I'd better get straight on with the morning review.'

'Good morning everyone, now can I have your attention please,' shouted the DCI across the room as he perched himself on the corner of one of the desks. The incident team gathered in a group across the front of the desk. 'Firstly, a warm welcome to the newly assigned officers who have joined us on this investigation. Hopefully with your help we can clear this one up quickly. You have all now had time to read the incident briefing notes that have been provided to yourselves, so I am not going through the scenario we have here, you will know by now the investigation is being known within the force as Operation Vanguard. Right straight on with it, someone must have seen something unusual at this scene being so close to the city and the river over a weekend. There are a couple of blocks of flats on the opposite side of the river in Lower Park Road and we need to start knocking on some doors as soon as possible, I am convinced someone must have witnessed something out of the ordinary. But first we need to draw up a door to door questionnaire. Tom, can you please put together a suitable questionnaire for officers to start this, you know the sort of things we need to ask.'

DC Nick Crowther from CID HQ had also now joined the team with responsibility for managing the actions and the tasks that lay ahead of them.

'Nick, glad you have joined us. Once we have the questionnaire from Tom, I want you to schedule all the door to door exercises. Make sure we don't repeat any visits, there's nothing worse than knocking on someone's door and finding an officer has already been there earlier. We don't want any duplication of those house to house calls, you will also need to include Souters Lane, Lower Bridge Street and all the areas around the Groves. Drag in any uniform resources you need to carry this out, I'll clear that with the boss so don't let anyone fob you off. As you know, the lady who found the body– Miss Agnes Middleton has already provided us with her statement but we need any information we can get from local residents particularly on the few days leading up to when the body was discovered on that Sunday morning. Someone must have seen something suspicious along that river bank. Derek, do we have any news yet on who the actual keyholder is for that particular boatshed?'

'Yes, we do sir,' replied DS Hinckley, 'a Mr Alfred Dixon who a few years ago ran a pleasure boating service from there, you know the sort of thing hiring of motorboats, rowing boats, pedalos, etc.'

'Pedalos! On the River Dee,' interjected PC Walker, 'things are looking up around here since I left the area, we might be having sunbeds and parasols next.'

'Well, maybe not pedalos,' replied DS Hinckley, 'Anyway he's away on a short holiday at present sir but he should be back any time. I've got an action to interview him on his return.'

'Any idea how long he has been gone Derek?'

'Yes sir, he flew out to Spain from Manchester Airport on the afternoon of Saturday 9th December.'

'Did he indeed. Right, thanks for that keep me informed.'

***

It hadn't taken DC Tom Harding long to come up with a set of standard questions that the house to house team would need to ask in visiting the properties in the immediate area. The team was also fortunately made up mainly of officers who were familiar with Queen's Park and Handbridge areas. Indeed, some of the uniformed officers regularly policed that part of the city.

For PC Martin Walker however it was a bit different and at one point he even thought he might have to buy himself a map.

***

Chester Police HQ – Major Incident Room
Two Days Later

The Operation Vanguard team had been busy all morning and finally returned to the incident room armed with mountains of paper from the House to House exercise. One by one each of the officers returned as arranged to the incident room in time for the afternoon briefing by the SIO.

PC Martin Walker was one of the last to return and came in almost gasping for air. He plonked himself down in a heap on the nearest chair, his eighteen-stone frame almost buckling the chair legs as he crashed down.

'I'm bloody exhausted after that, I can tell you I've walked some miles but met one or two interesting people particularly one at number 35. Just shows I've still got it, you never lose it you know.'

'Still got what?' replied one of officers.

'Sex appeal of course mate. I knocked at this door and this buxom woman I'd say about my age roughly, give or take a few years, comes to the door in a little pink negligee and a fag in her mouth. I mean it's almost midday for god's sake. Anyway, she invites me in for a cup of tea but I'm sure that's not what she was after. I tell you what mate there is no way I was stepping in there. Maybe she felt sorry for me.'

'Get off Walker, you are imagining it,' said DC Crowther who was busy sorting the questionnaires into investigative piles.

'No seriously, I know the signs mate and I think the old bushy moustache has something to do with it.'

'So did you go in then and have that erm so called cup of tea as you put it?'

'No fear mate. If you ask me, she's got what I would call a touch of furniture disease,' joked PC Walker.

'How do you mean?'

'Her chest was in her drawers!'

The entire incident room fell about laughter only to be halted by the DI who had just entered the incident room.

'That's quite enough of that Walker, I suggest you get on with your work before the SIO arrives,' shouted DS Hinckley

'Yes sir, sorry boss.'

***

Thursday, 14th December 1967, 09.00am

The Dixon family had arrived back from their brief Spanish holiday at Manchester Airport in the early hours. Ever since Alfred Dixon and his wife June had retired from their leisure boat business a couple of years ago, they always tried to get out to their favourite holiday destination of Torremolinos in the winter. They had arranged for Alfred's brother Alan to pick them up at the airport and they were now on the drive back on the A556 in the direction of Chester.

'So, you had a good time then Alfred? It looks as though the weather was good, you certainly have caught the sun,' said Alan as they passed through the village of Sandiway.

'Yes, spot on bruv, we could have done with staying longer but June had a last-minute hospital appointment to get back to. Anyway, it's always nice to have some sunshine in December, re-charge the old batteries and it sets you up for Christmas we always say. You should try it sometime. Anyway, what's being happening over here since we've gone?'

'Oh, nothing much, I can't think of anything really significant,' said Alan lying and shaking his head.

Alan Dixon had decided not to say anything to his brother and sister-in-law about the incident in Alfred's boathouse. He'd heard it all on the local radio and was pretty sure it was Alfred's old boathouse where the body had been found. Instead he thought he'd wait for them to get back home and settled in. As it happened when they finally pulled into Clwyd Avenue, Broughton the police were already waiting outside Alfred's house together with a few of the neighbours who were standing nearby wondering why the police car had been there all morning.

'What the hell has been going on here, we don't normally get a visit from the police down our street. It looks like one of the neighbours is in trouble by the look of it, bet it's those new ones who've just moved in,' exclaimed Alfred as the car came to a halt.

Alan said nothing and walked round to open the boot.

Alfred suddenly looked shocked as he was then approached by one of the police officers. He had just started to unload the two suitcases from the boot of the car.

'Mr Alfred Dixon?' enquired the uniformed police officer.

'Yes, that's right, is there a problem Officer? We haven't been burgled, have we? Has someone tried to break in?'

'No sir, you haven't been burgled, well as far as I am aware you haven't. Are you the still the owner of a boatshed near the Groves?' replied the police officer trying to dismiss Alfred's question.

'Yes, why has something happened there?'

The police officer didn't answer, meanwhile a small crowd of neighbours had appeared in their driveways straining to hear what was being said.

'Perhaps we could discuss this inside sir.'

'Yes, certainly Officer, come in, please come in.'

'It's okay Alan, you can leave us now, we'll soon clear this up, I'll talk to you later. Thanks ever so much for picking us up. I owe you one.'

Alan drove off he knew Alfred would be ringing him later on.

Alfred and his wife opened the front door and led the police officer into the front room.

'Would you like a cup of tea Officer,' said June who didn't seem bothered at all, 'I must admit we're quite parched, we haven't had a decent cup of tea since Malaga.'

'No thanks,' said the police officer as he removed his helmet and took a seat on the sofa.

'Very well Officer, please excuse me I need to unpack and get a brew going,' said June as she left the room.

The police officer just smiled and nodded.

'So Officer, what's all this about then, what's happened at the Boatshed? I haven't used it for a while, last time I was there kids had broken into it. I'm forever changing the lock on the damn place the sooner I get rid of it the better. I don't know why I still keep it to be honest,' said Alfred who was now panicking a bit.

'What time did you fly off to Spain sir?'

'Well, that would be about 1.30pm last Saturday afternoon.'

'So where were you on the Saturday a.m.?'

'Probably last-minute packing, here at home and getting ready for my brother Alan to take us to the airport. Look, what's all this about Officer. Has something happened at the boatshed?'

'Can someone confirm you were at home?'

'Yes of course, my wife.'

'So you haven't seen the news while you have been away sir?'

'No, I avoid it like the plague, I just like to get away from everything, I certainly don't buy a newspaper they are too expensive over there.'

'Well sir, there's been a young girl found murdered in your boatshed.'

Alfred went pale and sat down on the nearest chair.

'Who was she and when was this?'

'She was found on Sunday morning sir but we believe she was dumped there the day before.'

'Can anyone vouch that you were at home on the Saturday morning?'

'Yes, I told you, my wife can. I haven't been near the boatshed for weeks, we don't use it since we got rid of the small boats. I was hoping to sell it next spring in time for the summer season.'

'It's a murder scene now sir and is completely sealed off. Tell me sir, did anyone else have keys for the boatshed, ex-employees for example?'

'No,' he hesitated, 'well, yes, my staff used to have keys when we were running the business but as I say I've changed the locks since then.'

'Well, thank you for your time Mr Dixon, that will be all for now but we will be back in touch.'

Alfred was shaken, he showed the police officer to the door and slumped into the armchair.

***

Cheshire Police HQ Press Briefing
Friday, 15th December, 10.30am

The press piled into the first floor conference room at the Police HQ. No one had said anything on why they had been called in at short notice but each one of them knew there must have been some sort of a development in at least one of the two latest major incidents. The conference room was packed and somewhat noisy as DCI Sheraton and ACC Duckworth entered the briefing room and took their seats at the table.

As the ACC stood up suddenly all the chattering stopped as he began to address the press.

'Gentlemen, thank you for coming at such short notice. I have to tell you that we have now formally identified the girl's body that was found at that fire at Saughall a few weeks back. Through dental records she has now been identified as nineteen years of age Jennifer Webb who worked as a shop assistant in Saltney and also as a bar waitress in the city centre. Her mother and step father have been notified and our thoughts and prayers are with the family at this very sad time. Formal identification has now taken place and the police are appealing for any information particularly relating to Miss Webb's movements on the weekend of Saturday the 25th of November and Sunday 26th. Anyone with information then please contact the major incident room at Blacon Police station. Now DCI Sheraton and myself do have some time for a just a couple of questions.'

'James Albright – Deva Radio, at this point in time Detective Chief Inspector are you any closer to identifying the murderer?'

The DCI continued to sit whilst answering the question.

'Yes, we have a number of possible suspects and we are following a number of significant leads.'

'Can you elaborate on what you mean by "significant"?'

'No, I'm not prepared to go any further at this stage.'

'Have the family and next of kin been informed?'

'Yes, as I mentioned before we informed them last night and we ask that you please leave them alone at this very sad time, naturally they are very distressed.'

At this point the scruffy journalist from the previous press conference stood up.

'So are there any links between this incident and the woman's body that was found in that boatshed near the River Dee the other Sunday?'

'No, we do not believe they are linked but neither are we discounting that possibility.'

'Well, that sounds like a definite maybe to me if ever I heard one,' chuckled the journalist as he looked all around him for support with most of the press audience starting to burst into laughter.

The DCI was clearly rattled at this outburst but somehow managed to keep a calm head.

'Look, can I remind you we are investigating two murders at present, two young girls have lost their lives. At this stage we do not believe they are linked. If we should find through further investigation and subsequent evidence that they are in fact linked we will of course brief you all in a future press conference. Now are there any other questions?'

'Yes, Jim Edworthy – Wirral Gazette, have you identified the girl found in the boatshed yet?'

The DCI certainly wasn't going to get drawn into this a second time and the ACC had already indicated he would close the meeting.

'We are working on that Mr Edworthy. Now if there is nothing else this press conference is now closed. Thank you, gentlemen, for coming at such short notice.'

***

Blacon Incident Room
Friday, 15th December 1967, 2.00pm

When Michael Sheraton arrived back at Blacon, he found DC Blackwell standing precariously on a chair adding the final movements of Jennifer Webb in pencil to the timeline on the wall.

'Good afternoon John, you take it easy up there. I can see you've been busy already.'

'Yes sir, I'm going to have to rewrite this lot, it's getting a bit unreadable at present. Anyway, we've started by interviewing her boss at the shop where she worked full time in Saltney. His name is Norman Arrowsmith who co-incidentally we brought in for questioning the other day. DC Johnson interviewed him apparently, little did we realise at that point that Jennifer Webb was in fact our victim.'

'Ah yes, I remember Mr Arrowsmith coming in on suspicion of breaking and entering. He was snooping around the flats if I remember. Shifty looking character if you ask me. He's certainly on my radar!'

'Well, actually to be honest he's been quite helpful to us sir, he says Jennifer was actually working on the Saturday in the shop and he knew quite a bit about her friends and family contacts. We also now have a list of contacts from him that we need to follow up on.'

'Good, well let's hope we can piece together her movements on that particular weekend.

'DS Bradshaw, can you please follow up with the owners and staff at the club she worked at in the evenings and weekends? We need to know everything that went on during that Saturday evening, we now know she was working that night. I am particularly interested in interviewing her boss at that club. Also, assuming the J is Jennifer, we now need to know who the N is that was engraved as J&N on the back of the watch. I did ask Mr & Mrs Ellis, Jennifer's mother and step-father but they had no idea on who that could be which is a bit odd as you would have thought she would have at least mentioned it to them. Anyway, see what you can find out.'

'Yes sir, will do.'

'DC Blackwell, can you follow up on any other activity in the city that weekend. I suggest you start with the incident logs from the Command & Control system. You know the sort of thing we are after, disturbances, reports, calls to incidents etc. Let's see what was also going on around Saughall and of course the city centre that particular weekend.'

'Yes sir, I'm straight onto it.'

'DC Johnson, I'd like you to visit all the taxi companies in the city and get a list of drivers who were on duty that Saturday night. We then need to interview each one of them. They could well have seen something suspicious that we might not be aware of.'

'Will do sir.'

***

Beaumaris, Anglesey
Friday, 15th December 1967, 2.30pm

Nancy Ellis was still in a state of shock following the visit by DCI Sheraton and WPC Helen Williams yesterday evening who had confirmed Nancy's worst fears. The DCI also used the opportunity to show her the engraved watch and charm bracelet. She hadn't seen the bracelet before but confirmed it was indeed Jennifer's watch. Nancy couldn't throw any light however as to the engraving on the reverse of the watch. As far as Nancy could recall Jennifer hadn't had a steady boyfriend since she broke up with her old school friend Neil. Her husband Keith had also taken time off work to look after her but Nancy still refused to believe that it was her daughter that had been found in the remains of that fire. She still expected her to ring up anytime or cheerfully walk through the door unannounced like she used to. With no other family Nancy only had Keith to comfort her. The two of them sat there stunned in silence as they tried to come to terms with their loss.

'I haven't even cried Keith, well a proper cry anyway,' said Nancy as she sat in an armchair clutching an old school photograph of Jennifer, 'I mean why Jennifer, she was capable of looking after herself late at night. I simply can't take it in on how she was working on the Saturday day and night, then found on Monday morning like this. I just can't take it all in. Why our Jennifer?'

Keith shook his head and was simply stuck for words to comfort her but nevertheless placed his arms around her shoulder.

'Some Christmas this is going to be Keith, she was coming here to spend the holidays in Beaumaris with us. I was so looking forward to it. We've already even got her presents wrapped upstairs in the spare bedroom. Christmas will never ever be the same again.'

The silence continued with Nancy clutching the framed photograph to her breast.

Eventually Keith broke his silence.

'We'll get through this together love, you'll see.'

'I know but I can't take it all in, she was my only daughter, my only child, taken far too early.'

'Come on love, we will get through this and you have to face up to it, she's gone as hard as it seems. She wouldn't want you to be like this. Think of all the good times you had with her. All those nice memories of her when she was little.'

***

Chester City Centre
Friday, 15th December 1967, 8.30pm

This wasn't the first time that DS Bradshaw had visited the nightclub, not long after he had moved from the village of Northowram, near Halifax he had spent a few nights enjoying the live music that the club offered over the weekends. This was different for him on duty tonight however as he approached the barman.

'Excuse me is Mr Nigel Simpson working here this evening?'

'He might be and who wants to know?' said the long-haired barman in an aggressive tone of voice.

'DS Bradshaw from Cheshire Police wants to know,' as he flashed his warrant card.

'Oh right, yes, sorry about that Officer, I'll fetch him,' came the reply in a much-improved change of tone.

Minutes later the barman returned from the back office.

'I've told him, he said he shouldn't be long,' said the barman as he started to serve the queue of customers that had begun to form.

The DS took a seat at the end of the bar and waited for a while before Nigel Simpson eventually emerged behind the bar. He watched as the barman pointed the DS out.

'I gather you want to see me,' said Nigel Simpson with a puzzled sort of look.

'Yes, is there somewhere quieter that we can have a quick chat,' replied the DS as he showed his warrant card once again.

'Yes, follow me.'

The DS followed Nigel Simpson behind the bar into a small sparsely furnished office with no windows. The office consisting of a large old-fashioned oak desk, a small paraffin heater and two threadbare chairs which looked ready for the tip. Crates of empty beer bottles were stacked in one corner. On top of the desk was a pile of invoices which had been stacked through a spike indicating presumably that they had now been paid.

'Excuse the mess, I'm still having a tidy up. How can I help you Officer?'

'Did you know Jennifer Webb?'

'Yes, of course, she worked here part time until recently, good worker was Jennifer, very popular with the customers. Can't understand why she went off like that.'

'Like what exactly?'

'To be honest, she just packed the job in, not a word or anything, she was paid up to her last night here and that was the last we heard from her. It wasn't like her, I thought one of the customers might have upset her or something. I think she was finding it difficult to fit both jobs in to be honest. She worked at that grocery shop in Saltney full time I believe.'

'You haven't heard the news then Mr Simpson?'

'No what news?'

'I'm afraid to tell you that Jennifer is dead, she has been identified as the victim in that fire over at Saughall a few weeks back.'

Nigel's jaw dropped as he went into a state of shock flopping down on one of the chairs.

'I, I can't believe it, she was a lovely girl, I don't know what to say. I just don't know what to say.'

DS Bradshaw waited for a moment before continuing.

'Can I ask you to cast your mind back to the weekend of 25th November Mr Simpson, was there anything that happened out of the norm over that weekend, probably the Saturday night, an incident in the club perhaps that you can think of?'

'No, I don't think so. We are a well-run club with hardly any bother. Our security guys keep a close eye on possible troublemakers, they are turfed out as soon as there is any sign of trouble. This is a shock, I can't believe it, who would do such a thing she was a lovely girl.'

'Have you ever seen her wearing these?'

The DS showed him photographs of the bracelet and watch including the engraving.

Nigel Simpson shook his head, 'Can't say I have, no. Did they belong to her?'

The DS nodded, 'Well, if anything does come to mind please call us at the incident room, the number is on here,' replied the DS as he handed him a business card.

'I'm in shock, I can tell you and I know the rest of the staff will be when they find out.'

'Yes, I'm sure they will, thanks I'll see myself out. Oh just one more thing did you ever visit Jennifer's flat?'

'No, I can't say I have.'

DS Bradshaw made his way out into the bar area and left the club by the side door but couldn't help thinking there was something that Nigel Simpson wasn't telling him.

***

Blacon Incident Room – Saturday, 16th December, 10.00am

DC Johnson didn't waste any time in contacting all the taxi companies in the city centre and every one of them had been most helpful in providing him with lists of drivers who had been on duty during that weekend of 25th and 26th November. Even though it was just a few weeks before Christmas he was surprised at the number of drivers who had been working that weekend and decided to concentrate on those drivers who had been working late on the Saturday evening after all he knew from Norman Arrowsmith's statement that Jennifer Webb had been working most of the day at the grocery shop. As he glanced down the long list, he saw one name in particular that jumped out at him. Bill Newton from Ellesmere Port. He remembered the name and the address from a couple of years back where he had attended an incident. A woman had reported her husband to the police for threatening her with a bread knife. He remembered visiting the house and, in the end, she had decided not to press charges. DC Johnson marked the sheet with an asterisk and continued browsing down the list.

Chapter 12

Ellesmere Port
Monday, 18th December 1967, 10.30am

DC Johnson had no trouble finding the house, it immediately brought back memories of that night a couple of years ago as he stood there ringing the doorbell. At first it looked like no one was at home, he'd noticed however that the curtains were drawn upstairs. He continued to ring the bell and minutes later a scruffy man with a grey unkempt beard in his sixties came to the front door. Although he was dressed in jeans and tee shirt with no shoes he looked as though he'd just got out of bed.

'Yes, what do you want,' said the man rubbing his eyes and having difficulty to focus.

'Mr Newton, Mr Bill Newton?' enquired DC Johnson.

'Yes, what of it? If you have a parcel to deliver for those across the road you can leave it round the back of their house, they are always ordering stuff from catalogues, damn nuisance as they always try and deliver them here for some sodding reason.'

'I'm DC Johnson, Cheshire Police I wonder if you could spare me a few minutes?' he said flashing his warrant card.

'Well, I've just got out of bed, can't it wait. I was working late last night in Chester city centre. I need to catch up on my sleep before getting back to work this afternoon.'

'Yes, I'm sorry to disturb you Mr Newton but it is quite important.'

'Aye, well I expect you'd better come in then.'

DC Johnson entered the hallway and remembered the last time he had visited there but this time the house was different somehow. As he entered the lounge, he then realised what was different, there was now hardly any furniture in there, it was almost bare with just two armchairs and a small TV and portable radio in the corner. A beige rug in front of the fire looked as though it had been burnt several times presumably from coal spitting out from the open fireplace. Bill Newton took a seat in the armchair closest to the unlit fire and DC Johnson sat opposite in the vacant chair.

'You may remember me visiting you a couple of years ago Mr Newton, I attended an incident here involving you and your wife.'

'Good god, you haven't come about that have you, I thought I recognised you, you were in uniform then. That was all resolved, she's cleared off back to her new boyfriend and good riddance is what I damn well say. She did me a bloody favour?' retorted Bill Newton looking shocked.

'No, no, not at all nothing to do with that incident. Mr Newton. I understand you were working as a taxi driver in Chester City Centre on the weekend of 25th and 26th November?'

'Was I? Probably I'd have to check my works diary and get back to you on that one.'

'Well, your office told me you were.'

'Well, if they said I was, then I must have been. What's so special about that weekend anyway, that's nearly a month ago?'

'Well sir, a girl who had been working in one of the clubs on the Saturday evening was found murdered on the Monday morning. Can you recall anything out of the ordinary on that Saturday night particularly say around midnight?'

'Now, you've got me there,' said Bill Newton stroking his chin and taking a sharp intake of breath, 'I'd need to have a think about that. As you can imagine Saturdays are always busy for us lot. There was something a few weeks back with a youth if I remember, what was it now? Aye that's right he wanted a lift to Buckley, not sure if that's the same weekend, seems about the same time. He was in a right state, vomiting everywhere and kicking my cab tyres. He ran off down an alley by the cathedral I think, well stumbled to be precise. There was no way I was letting him into the cab.'

DC Johnson continued to write down on his notepad and paused for a short while before continuing.

'Well, could you describe him?'

'No, not really it was dark and it was a few weeks ago I'm afraid. I'd struggle there. I guess he'd be about eighteen years, dark hair, bit scruffy, dark clothes and probably about 5'6 at a guess.'

'What time did you finish that night?'

'It must have been straight after I'd seen that youth.'

'And did you go straight home?'

'No, I went back to the taxi office, had a brew with a couple of the lads before heading home I think.'

'Okay well thanks Mr Newton, if you do think of anything here's my card, give me a ring at Blacon Police station.'

Chapter 13

Chester
Saturday 23rd December 1967

Mike Sheraton had been up early this morning to make the journey across to Colwyn Bay to pick his mother Edith up so she could spend a few days with them in Chester over Christmas.

As he pulled back the bedroom curtains half expecting to see a hint of a snowfall, he saw that it was raining heavily. *There goes the white Christmas, well at least the roads will be clear,* he thought to himself. Mike had promised he would do his level best to at least spend some time with the family over Christmas. The roads had been much busier than normal with last minute shoppers and people heading home for the holidays. As he arrived at the smart apartment block just outside Old Colwyn overlooking the bay, he couldn't help but notice that his mother was already sat in the reception lounge area with her coat on and not one but three large suitcases stacked up in the hallway. It was always good to see his mum and with work pressures he rarely found the time to get over to see her.

'Bang on time as always Michael, always as punctual as your father,' she said as he walked into the foyer, 'I've only been sat here five minutes, I thought I'd get one of the neighbours to help me down with the luggage.'

'It's good to see you Mum,' he said as they hugged each other, 'but how long are you planning to stop, there's enough packed in here for a month!'

'Well, you never know with the weather changing I always like to have several changes of clothes and of course your presents are in one of the cases. I've been so looking forward to spending Christmas with you all. Now then, are you going to stop for a cup of tea first or shall we have a coffee break en-route?'

'No, I'll have to get straight back to work Mum, as I've got a pretty busy day back in the office today.'

'I've told you before, it's about time you retired our Michael, you need to enjoy life and then perhaps come over and stay with me for a few days. We're only on this planet once you know. It's about time you hung up your boots or whatever it is you ex coppers do!'

'Yes Mum, I can see Jane has been talking to you.'

Mike loaded the cases in the car and they headed straight back to Chester, this time down the old coast road. The journey back took longer with traffic heading into the city centre and it was much busier than normal even though it was a Saturday.

Mike dropped his mother off at home in Rowton and then had to shoot back into the office for a review with the Blacon investigation team. As he entered the incident room, he was greeted by DC Johnson coming out of the kitchen with a tray of mince pies.

'Care for a mince pie sir, John's wife Margaret has made them herself?'

'I will indeed, yes, thanks Peter. I must admit I'm quite peckish, I had an early start and no breakfast.'

'Any chance of a coffee anyone?' he muttered through eating a mouthful of mice pie, 'Hmm, very tasty John, tell Mrs Blackwell she is an excellent baker, she certainly gets my vote.'

'Will do sir and coffee is on its way.'

DCI Sheraton walked over to the flip chart stand and started scribing out a number of names.

'Good afternoon chaps, if we can just get started, I want to understand where we currently are with the investigation. Firstly, where are we with the taxi driver lists?'

'Well sir, we've interviewed all of the ones working on that Saturday night. Most had a typical night nothing out of the ordinary apart from Bill Newton from Ellesmere Port. He went into some detail on a problem youth he came across late at night not far from the cathedral. Apparently, this lad who was very drunk went off in the direction of the nightclub where Jennifer Webb was working. It was a lad from Buckley apparently, we have a basic description but not much to go on I'm afraid.'

'And what about Bill Newton himself, do you think he's invented this youth from Buckley?' asked the DCI, 'Didn't I read somewhere that he had assaulted his wife in the past?'

'Yes, that's right sir but I don't think he had anything to do with this.'

'And what makes you say that?'

'Just a hunch sir, and he said he was working until after midnight, then he went home after first calling in at the taxi office over at Christleton. He said he was sat in there talking to one or two of the other drivers and the call operator until the early hours.'

'But he was working in the area by the cathedral, he could have already put Jennifer's body in the boot of his car, then gone to Christleton for an alibi.' exclaimed DI Smethurst.

'True,' nodded the DCI, 'did you check his alibi?'

'No sir, it's on my list.'

'Okay, well do that as soon as possible. Moving on, Nigel Simpson at the nightclub, what have we found on him?'

'Seems a decent enough sort of bloke sir, good manager I believe, runs a busy club, very efficient,' interjected DS Bradshaw, 'although when I interviewed him, I wasn't sure he was telling me everything, he seemed to be holding back on something.'

'How do you mean sergeant?'

'I think he had something to hide sir, there was something about his relationship with Jennifer. I asked him had he ever seen the bracelet and the watch before. He behaved strangely at this saying he hadn't seen them before which I find hard to believe. I'm sure Jennifer would have been wearing these items in work that night.'

'Yes, that's a fair point and he would have been one of the last to see her on that Saturday night.'

'So now we come to Norman Arrowsmith, where are we with our Mr Arrowsmith?'

'Well sir,' said DC Blackwell, 'DC Johnson and myself have interviewed him a couple of times, he was quite helpful to be honest, he gave us details on where Jennifer worked, family contacts, friends etc. He seemed to know quite a lot about her, too much to be honest. I think he had a thing about her, fancied her if you ask me. I got that impression and he was found looking through her lounge window of course. Was he planning to break in after he'd murdered her? Perhaps to remove evidence of some kind. Did he murder her in her own flat for example and then dump her body afterwards?'

'And he did drive a grey Morris Minor!' interjected DC Johnson who had certainly taken a dislike to Norman Arrowsmith.

'Yes, I'd forgotten about the grey Morris Minor, we think this was the type of car spotted in the city centre and down Lodge Lane.'

'Have we examined his car?'

'Yes, we've been right through it sir, some evidence of blood which checks out with his own blood group and not Jennifer Webb's blood group from her medical records. He said he cut himself dismantling his mother's conservatory.'

'Hmm, of course forensics have also been through her flat with a fine-tooth comb and there's nothing there to alert us. She was probably murdered elsewhere in my view.'

'Now the one I'm still interested in is Jim Adams, where are we with him?'

'Right sir,' said DS Bradshaw, 'I've spoken with Jim Adams, if you recall he was the farmworker that was ill over that weekend. He seemed perfectly well as far I was concerned but I did check and Jim had been to see his Doctor complaining of a stomach problem, he'd been diagnosed with food poisoning apparently. So highly unlikely he made the trip into Chester.'

'Thanks Peter.'

'And of course we do have Kenneth Smith on our list, from the farm although I think we can strike him off now. I'm satisfied he was over at Saltney with that woman, his so-called girlfriend! That brings us onto the incidents that weekend, what do we know?' asked the DCI as he struck a line through some of the names on the flip chart.

'Well sir, looking through the incident logs there was a report of screaming not far from St Werburgh Street. I followed it up with the gentleman who reported it and he couldn't tell us much more than we already know. No one else reported anything suspicious.'

'What time was this?' asked the DCI who was now busy studying the timeline across the wall.

'About 12.30 on the Sunday morning sir.'

'There's nothing on here about that, come on, let's keep it updated chaps otherwise we are going to miss something. Okay well that will be all for now. I'm heading back to the office. Keep up the good work and if you have time to celebrate Christmas, then have a good one. I'm pretty sure we'll be seeing each other in here over the break.'

***

Rowton
Monday, 25th December 1967, 11.50am

The Sheratons had been up bright and early this morning, opening their Christmas presents before breakfast and then heading off to church.

This was the first time that Mary Sheraton had been back to Rowton church since moving away to Colwyn Bay and she had been really looking forward to seeing her old friends in the church. Everyone made a huge fuss of her at the end of the service that they almost had a job to get back in time for lunch.

'I must say grandma, you certainly received a big welcome back at the church this morning,' said Janet as she poured the sherry for the traditional Christmas toast, 'I didn't think we would get back here in time to toast absent friends.'

The Sheraton family always followed a family tradition of toasting their friends and family far and near at midday every Christmas day.

'Yes, it was good to be back at the old church, they were very supportive when dear old John passed away,' replied Edith who was helping Jane in the kitchen.'

'Come on everybody, else you'll miss the annual toast!' shouted Mike as he raised his glass.

Edith and Jane came rushing in from the kitchen.

'Absent Friends,' said Mike Sheraton as the other three echoed the toast.

'Pity your parents couldn't make it Jane,' said Edith as she finished her sherry.

'Yes, it is Mum, still they'll be on the phone later on and with a bit of luck we will get to see them in the new year.'

They all returned to their various chores in the kitchen and the dining room.

'So have you got a good Christmas break this time Mike?' asked Edith as she brought in the plates.

'Afraid not Mum, it's back to the office for me tomorrow. With a bit of luck though, I should be here most evenings.'

'I suppose you will be watching the Queen's broadcast today Mum?' said Mike as he laid the table in readiness for the Christmas Day lunch.

'I will indeed Mike, it's in colour for the very first time, I'm looking forward to it. I assume we'll all be watching it together?'

'He'll probably be asleep by then,' laughed Jane, 'after he's had a couple of glasses of wine at lunchtime.'

'And the rest,' laughed Janet.

***

Tuesday, 26th December 1967, 8.00am

'I'm sorry to trouble you at home so early sir, but there has been a bit of a development.'

'That's fine Peter, I was already up and planning to come into today anyway. So what's new?' replied Mike Sheraton who was about to go into the bathroom when the phone call came in.

'It's that Taxi driver sir, remember the one from Ellesmere Port – his name is Bill Newton.'

'Yes, what about him?'

'Well, we were checking out his alibi and he couldn't possibly have gone back to the taxi office on that particular night. They closed at midnight apparently something to do with the call handling operator being ill. She'd locked up and gone home, she remembers it well, it was her son's birthday the same day.'

'Right, well we need to get Mr Newton into the station as soon as possible, Christmas or no Christmas.'

'I think there's a bit more to it sir, we found out late last night that Bill Newton attempted to commit suicide yesterday afternoon. A neighbour who was inviting him over for a Christmas drink found him apparently on the floor he'd taken an overdose. They got to him just in time I believe, he's recovering in the Royal Infirmary.'

'Good god, is he alright?'

'Yes, he should be fine.'

'Right, I'll get into the incident room as soon as I can.'

Mike Sheraton didn't hang about, he got washed and dressed in record time and headed out to Blacon. The roads were naturally quiet although the city centre traffic seemed almost normal as shoppers headed for the Boxing day sales. He arrived at the Blacon incident room in record time. DS Bradshaw was already on the phone to the hospital.

The DCI waited for him to finish his phone call.

'Just been onto the Matron at the hospital guv to get an update, he's awake a bit groggy and they are planning to keep him in overnight. I told her we would be in this morning to see him and she didn't seem best pleased.'

'Well, let's get over there Peter, I'll drive.'

The DCI and DS didn't waste any time and twenty minutes later they were at ward six in the hospital. Bill Newton was in a private room within the ward and was awake when the two detectives entered. He was propped up on two pillows in a half sleeping position. As they approached him, he opened his eyes briefly.

'Who are you two then?' said Bill Newton half expecting that they were doctors about to examine him.

'DCI Sheraton and DS Bradshaw, we'd like to ask you a few questions Mr Newton.'

'Good god is nowhere safe? I told that officer the other day everything I remember from that night. I assume that's what you are here about?'

'We'd just like to clarify one or two things with you Mr Newton, you said after finishing on that night you went back to the taxi office.'

'Yes, that's right.'

'And you had a brew with two other taxi drivers?'

'Yes, that's right

'But that's not right is it Mr Newton, the office was closed that night at midnight, so where exactly did you go afterwards?' replied the DCI.

Bill Newton looked stunned for a minute.

'Mr Newton, well where did you go?'

'Erm, I must have been mistaken, it might have been a different night. It was a while ago you know.'

'So let me take you back to that night in question, was that the actual night that you saw that youth from Buckley that you mentioned?'

'I can't be sure. I think so, you are making me think now.'

'Did that youth really exist Mr Newton or is it a figment of your imagination?'

Bill Newton started to get irate.

'Yes of course he existed, I'm not imagining things you know.'

'Why did you take an overdose Mr Newton? Is there something you are not telling us?'

'Well, I was depressed,' he sighed, 'I wasn't looking forward to another lonely Christmas and didn't seem to have anything to live for anymore. I had a drink or two, got the whisky bottle out and then decided life wasn't worth living. I took a few tablets and next thing must have fallen asleep. I don't remember anything until waking up here in hospital.'

Suddenly Bill Newton looked exhausted and just then, the matron who had been watching from the ward window intervened from the adjoining ward.

'Now I'm sorry officers I think that's quite enough for now. Mr Newton needs some rest now. Can I ask you to please continue this tomorrow?'

The DCI nodded to DS Bradshaw and they made their way down to the stairs to the car park.

'What do you think boss?'

'I'm not convinced, he's still on my list.' sighed the DCI.

Chapter 14

Monday, 1ˢᵗ January 1968, 6.45am

With his head still under the bedclothes Mike Sheraton reached out to switch off the alarm clock and knocked it flying off the bedside table hitting the wall in the process as it continued to ring out.

'Sorry about that love, I'll get you a cup of tea in a minute,' he mumbled as he struggled to get one foot out of bed.

Jane didn't hear any of it, she was in another world, out like a light and quietly snoring away to herself.

It had only seemed like minutes that he'd been in bed after Jane and himself had attended a New Year's Eve dinner with close friends over at Tarvin. Previously in the day Mike had dropped his mother back home at Colwyn Bay, she always preferred to be at home for New Year. They stayed in Tarvin to see the new year in watching Andy Stewart and Kenneth McKellar in the White Heather club on the TV. Jane had then driven them home just after 1am and Mike had decided to have one or two more nightcaps before finally retiring. He'd woke this morning with a blinding headache. It was a normal work day and he'd wished in hindsight that he had booked it off but he knew the answer that he would have got from his boss with two currently undetected murders on his hands.

He sat on the edge of the bed for a few minutes, his head was throbbing and he was almost afraid of standing up.

'Oh, my bloody head, I must have had a dodgy pint beforehand.'

There was no response from Jane, just a slight snore under the bed covers.

He replaced the alarm clock on the bedside table and edged his way very slowly across the window ledge into the en-suite bathroom. As he took a quick look in the bathroom mirror, he realised he looked dreadful and promised himself he would not get in that state ever again, something he had promised so many times in the past. After a warm shower, a shave, a large mug of hot tea and two aspirins at least he felt ready to attempt to make his way into work. The weather was fine, crisp but very cold and it took him a few minutes to de-ice the windscreen. Some thirty minutes later he arrived at HQ. As he entered the office, he was somewhat surprised to see all his team in as usual hard at it busy writing up the index cards from the house to house questionnaire exercise that they had just completed just two days before.

'Good morning boss and a Happy New Year to you!' shouted DS Hinckley from the small kitchen area, 'The kettle's on, I guess you could do with a brew.'

'Good morning to you, yes please and a happy new year to you all, pleased you've all made it in on time,' he replied, 'although why on earth New Year's Day isn't a bank holiday is beyond me. It would have made for a great long weekend. Anyway, it is as it is. Good to see you all in here. So let's get started there's no point in being miserable about it.'

The DCI sat down and started leafing through his in tray, most of it was internal post including the usual case progress notes from other incidents in his area together with the officers reports he's requested from the Blacon incident room. But at the bottom of the pile there was a badly written envelope marked personal and confidential addressed to himself. He was curious, it was postmarked Wrexham, he carefully opened up the envelope and removed the letter which looked at first glance that a child had written it.

Dear DCI Sheraton

I trust you and your team had a busy Christmas!

I see that you are no nearer finding me. Yes, I bet even with the help of Scotland Yard you still wouldn't be able to catch me. I was just too clever for you. Well, enjoy your retirement whenever that happens and rest easy knowing that I'm still out there, somewhere and maybe just maybe I might just strike again!

Who knows?

Regards
Fire and Water

The DCI was almost tempted to rip it up immediately but knew that the envelope and the letter had to be kept on file as evidence, he called DS Hinckley over and handed him the letter. He trusted Derek completely, they had worked on so many cases, he was the officer Mike Sheraton had the most trust in.

'Do you think this really is from our offender boss?'

'It's possible. I've seen this sort of thing before, it could be genuine but there are some strange people out there who just like to keep us on our toes Derek. To be honest I don't know what to think.'

'Anyway, where's he got the idea that you are planning to retire boss?'

'Well, that's a mystery to me but keep this to yourself,' replied the DCI as he filed the letter.

***

Liverpool Daily Post
Tuesday, 2nd January 1968

A young man's body was found on Monday night in a green Morris Minor car parked in a side road at Denbigh according to North Wales police.

Authorities are waiting on autopsy results in the death of the man, identified as 18-year-old Stephen Derek Longshaw (also known as Sid Longshaw) from Buckley, Flintshire. The cause of death will be determined by the local pathologist Dr Henry Thomas.

Murder detectives were uncertain at this stage whether any foul play was involved.

Detectives said an elderly gentleman walking back from the pub found the young man around 7:30 p.m. on New Year's Day slumped in his vehicle at the junction between Ruthin Road and Hewitt's Lane. The body could have been there for at least a "couple of days", detectives said.

Anyone with information is asked to please contact the North Wales Police.

***

Wednesday, 3rd January 1968

The sun was just coming up on what promised to be a clear bright and frosty morning when DCI Sheraton came down for breakfast. Jane had already been up before him as she couldn't sleep and was busy cooking breakfast for the three of them.

'What a grand morning, it makes you glad to be alive. Anyway, you are up early love,?' said Mike Sheraton as he stood in front of the dining room mirror tying his tie.

'Yes, I couldn't sleep last night, I'm sorry if I disturbed you love.'

'Didn't hear a thing love, I had the best night's sleep for a long time. Anyway, I've been called into see ACC Duckworth first thing this morning. Don't know what that's all about he probably wants an update on things. Can't really tell him much more than he already knows to be honest. And before you ask no, this is not the time for me to mention my retirement.'

'You must be a mind reader Mike Sheraton,' laughed Jane as she continued to set out the breakfast table, 'well, at least one thing's certain, it is going to be this year!'

'Yes, that's true, hadn't thought about that, just let me clear these two cases up first. I will get around to it I promise.'

'No sign of Janet appearing yet?' said Mike as he poured himself a coffee.

'No, I've shouted her once, I'll go up in a minute to see if she's awake.'

Mike sat for a while thinking on how best to progress the two cases. He finished his breakfast as quickly as he could, put on his overcoat, grabbed his briefcase and left the house. He scraped the windscreen and set off for the city centre.

One hour later Mike Sheraton had arrived at his office in HQ. He had only been sat down at his desk for two minutes when the phone rang.

'Good morning, whenever you're ready Mike, we need to have that chat,' said the ACC from across the corridor.

'I'll be there straight away sir.'

The DCI made his way across the corridor and knocked on the door just to make sure the ACC wasn't in discussion with anyone.

'Come in, come in Mike,' shouted the ACC who was leafing through the morning newspaper, 'sit yourself down.'

Mike Sheraton closed the door behind him and took a seat at the ACC's conference table.

'So Mike, I've been quite impressed with how you've been handling those two major incident cases recently. God knows, it certainly couldn't have been easy balancing your workload across the two incident room locations. Yes, very impressed indeed, just hope we can start seeing some results soon.'

'Thank you, sir, that's kind of you to say.'

'Yes, and that's why I am arranging for you to have some additional help. God knows you've deserved it, only the other day the chief remarked to me that you should have additional help and I'm in complete agreement with him.'

'Thank you, sir, I must admit we could certainly do with some extra resources at present.'

'Good, so on the advice from the Chief I've arranged for one of the DCI's in the Met to come up and join you until we get a result on these two cases. Good to know isn't it that I can still pull a few strings back at my old force.'

'Erm, yes sir.'

Mike was stunned and far from happy with the situation, he'd expected additional resources from within his own force to assist him but not someone from New Scotland Yard. He immediately thought back to that anonymous letter he had received which actually mentioned help from Scotland Yard. He decided to speak up.

'But sir, I don't…'

'No there's no need to thank me Mike,' interrupted the ACC waving his hand, 'you deserve to have the best resource available and the new man comes highly recommended.'

'So, when will this new DCI arrive sir?'

'His name is DCI Pipe and should be with you tomorrow. He's arriving into Chester by train first thing, we've booked him into the Blossoms temporarily until we find him something more permanent. I know you two will get on well and hopefully we can clear up these cases pronto. Well, if there's nothing else Mike I'll see you tomorrow morning for the briefing when he's arrived.'

The ACC signalled the meeting was now over by continuing to leaf through the newspaper as if he was looking for something specific.

DCI Sheraton was gutted, he hadn't expected this and for one moment thought this could be the time to tell the ACC he was retiring, in the end he took a deep breath and returned swiftly to his office. He'd only been there for five minutes and was deep in thought on how he would work with this new

DCI. He hadn't even noticed his secretary Helen come in with the morning post.

'Good morning sir, the usual reports today plus a badly written envelope postmarked Mold, Flintshire, whoever has sent it,' laughed Helen as she placed the pile on his desk, 'they couldn't even spell Cheshire correctly.'

'Oh, sorry Helen, I was miles away, yes, good morning. Thanks for this,' replied the DCI as he started working through the pile of post. He soon came across the brown envelope marked for his attention. Helen was right, it was a wonder the letter had even arrived at Police HQ. It was marked "For the attention of the senior murder detective, Chesshere Police", no other address. The DCI carefully opened the envelope and pulled out the grubby letter that was folded inside. It had been written on what looked to have been a page ripped out from a school exercise book.

The letter was different from the one he had received the other day and the DCI was convinced this one was from a different person. It read as follows:

Dear Senior Investigating Officer

I note you still haven't made any arrests and I am amazed you and your team can detect anything. I wouldn't pay them in washers. It's about time you got some additional help, some real detectives on the case. In the meantime, the killer is still out there and you're still sitting on your arse and by the sound of it nowhere near catching him! You lot are quite simply as useful as trying to hold five pounds of shit in a three-pound bag!

Regards
An annoyed taxpayer

The DCI smiled at the expression, filed the letter and envelope and continued with reading the rest of the post. He thought it was an amazing co-incidence the letter referred to "additional help", somebody in the know or had this actually come from someone internally, someone with a grudge in the force. He dismissed the idea, he had enough on his plate without taking any notice of that letter, he'd seen a lot worse. He still hadn't got over that the ACC had brought in another DCI. He could almost understand it if it had been another senior officer from his own force but one from the Met!

He swivelled his chair round and stared at the bleak scene outside, not a single leaf on any of the trees. From his office window he could see the Chester horse racing track and beyond it the River Dee. January was already starting to make its mark, getting much colder at nights and in a couple of weeks the snows would arrive which always created a magical scene from his office window. Mike sat there pondering on how he should deal with the new DCI. He suddenly had a thought and picked up the phone.

'Hi Derek, do you fancy a pint at lunch time?'

'Yes, sure thing sir, what's the special occasion?'

'Nothing special I just need a pint and a chat, just the two of us you understand, meet you in the local say about 12.30.

'Look forward to it sir.'

***

Ye Olde Custom House Inn – 3rd January 1968, 12.25

Mike Sheraton pushed open the door of the pub and he was surprised to see Derek Hinckley already standing there at the bar. The bar was quiet with just a couple of elderly gentlemen reading newspapers at a table over by the window. The barmaid was just placing the last pint on the bar.

'Just got you one in sir!' exclaimed Derek as he handed over the pint of bitter.

'It's Mike here, Derek, no need for the sir, it's a social occasion.'

Mike Sheraton and Derek Hinckley had known each other for years, both had joined the force around the same time and had worked together on many high-profile cases. Mike had complete trust in him and vice versa.

'So Mike, are you going to tell me what the occasion is about, it's not often we get down the pub together these days, not your birthday is it?'

Mike took a large mouthful before responding and he'd already noticed the barmaid eavesdropping on their conversation.

'No, nothing like that, let's take a seat over there Derek, it's a bit sensitive.'

The two detectives took their drinks and found a seat in the far corner. Mike Sheraton paraphrased the meeting that he had had earlier with the ACC.

'I'm shocked Mike as I'm sure you are, it's early days yet on the boatshed incident. What makes the ACC think that one of the Met guys can spot things that we wouldn't?'

'I agree Derek, I'm far from happy with the situation. Be interesting to see how our own officers will react to this outsider coming in.'

The two carried on discussing how they could work with the new DCI and get the best out of the situation.

***

Later that same day.

Jane Sheraton was surprised to see Mike arriving home earlier than normal. In fact, she thought he might be unwell as he had looked exhausted over the past couple of weeks.

'You are home early love,' she shouted as he walked down the hallway, passing the oak staircase and almost throwing his car keys on the hall table,' is everything alright love? I've just got the kettle on, but I'm afraid supper won't be ready for a good hour or two yet but I can always make us a brew. Sit yourself down I've lit the fire in the front room.'

'No tea thanks, I need a stiff drink love,' he replied as he entered the lounge. The open fire was roaring away, he was so glad to be at home. He opened the cocktail cabinet to search for the bottle of malt whisky he'd just had as a Christmas present from his mother.'

'It's a bit early Mike but being as you are having one, I'll join you. After all I can't let you drink on your own.'

Mike poured the two whiskies using the best crystal cut glasses from the cabinet, handed one to Jane who had just finished in the kitchen and flopped himself down in his favourite armchair besides the log fire.

'Do you know what love,' he said taking a mouthful of whisky, 'I think it really is time for me to retire. I always remember an old sergeant of mine, Bill Oldfield was his name, telling me, *"Do you know lad, you will know when it's time to finish,"* and I think he was dead right. I think that time has arrived. I shall tell old Duckworth in the morning he can shove his job.'

'Eh, what's brought all this on Mike, I haven't seen you like this for a long time? You seemed okay when you went out this morning in fact you were looking forward to going to work.'

'Well, you won't believe this, old Duckworth has decided to call in the Met to work on both cases. There's a new DCI coming in tomorrow to help us with the two incidents. I mean he hasn't given us enough time, I'm sure we are starting to get somewhere with both of them.'

'Come on, that's not all bad news Mike, I mean he'll be helpful to you surely, it gives you a bit of cover and you can take the odd day off, it'll do you good, another pair of hands.'

'I suppose you're right love, maybe I'll think differently in the morning.'

***

Cheshire Police HQ, Major Incident Room
Thursday, 4th January 1968, 9.00am

The Operation Vanguard incident room was as busy as ever with officers following up on the recent request to the public for any information on the suspicious vehicle that had been parked on Souters Lane. They had received several calls mentioning a grey car, with one caller saying that she had seen the driver arguing with a young girl on the Saturday morning, the day before the body was found. Word had also now got around that the team would be joined by a new DCI from New Scotland Yard and rumours had already started on whether an entire new investigation team would actually take over the two incidents.

'So when's this new bloke arriving anyway?' said PC Walker as he took his empty mug over to the tea pot.

'Which new bloke? Oh, you mean DCI Pipe from the Met, he should be with us today that's what I've heard anyway.'

'I just hope his first name isn't Dwayne then,' said PC Walker with a wry smile on his face as he poured himself a mug of tea.

'How d'you mean, I'm not with you?' replied DC Crowther looking up from the card index trays.

'Well, he'd be known as Inspector Dwayne Pipe in the yard!' laughed PC Walker.

'Trust you to think of something like that Walker, haven't you got anything better to do than dream these things up.'

The laughter quickly subsided as DS Hinckley entered the room.

'This place looks as though a bomb has hit it,' bellowed the DS, 'let's at least have a tidy up chaps before the new DCI arrives. I realise with mountains of paper and index cards to wade through it's difficult but let's not give the DCI from the Met the wrong impression eh.'

***

DCI Sheraton had been in his office earlier than normal this morning, he needed to prepare for the briefing for DCI Pipe's arrival. Somehow, he felt better than he had yesterday, he told himself not to rush into things. In some ways to Mike Sheraton it felt like a handover of responsibility but of course it wasn't that at all. He had to keep reminding himself that DCI Pipe was here to help the force with the investigation of both incidents and in some ways the quicker they got the results the sooner he could finally hand his ticket in and take that retirement he'd been so looking forward to. A pair of fresh eyes on both investigations could also prove useful just in case they have missed something. He was now running late and just putting the final touches to the hand written document ready for typing when the ACC Crime burst into Mike's office.

'Mike, I've just had a phone call, he's running late apparently, he's missed the train from Euston somehow but he said he should be with us early afternoon. Not a good start you'll agree but at least it gives you a bit more time to prepare for him.'

The ACC returned to his office and Mike Sheraton was slightly relieved, at least he had a few more hours to complete the briefing document. He'd decided as discussed with DS Hinckley he would brief DCI Pipe just purely on the Blacon incident first and leave him with the incident team over there rather than confusing him with both enquiries.

***

Cheshire Police HQ, 2.15pm

'DCI Pipe to see you sir, he's waiting in reception.'
'Thanks Helen, I'll be straight down to bring him up.'
DCI Sheraton took the lift to the ground floor and walked over to the reception area. He hadn't known what to expect but he was somewhat surprised when the tall well dressed, grey haired giant of a man stood up and walked towards him. DCI Pipe certainly looked the part in a navy suit, white shirt,

blue striped tie, matching handkerchief, and polished black shoes that you could see your face in.

'Welcome to Cheshire Police HQ, glad you finally made it,' said DCI Sheraton as the two men shook hands. DCI Pipe was a huge man, probably about the same age as Mike Sheraton with hands the size of shovels. Mike thought he must have definitely been a number 4 or 5 in a rugby union side in his time. Sheraton was by no means short but even he was dwarfed by him.

'Ray Pipe, good to meet you, Mike isn't it?'

'Yes, good to meet you. We'll take the lift and grab a coffee on the way. Did you have a good journey in the end?'

The two men made their way from reception, continued their conversation about the train journey and the weather until they had reached the lift.

'Yes, well after that taxi problem in the city, I missed the damn train so I'm sorry about that I should have been here this morning. Anyway, it did give me some time to read up on the two murder cases you have on the go. Your ACC Crime had kindly sent me a briefing note in the post which I got yesterday so I feel I know at least something about these cases.'

Mike Sheraton thought to himself old Duckworth had done it once again, duplicated the work in writing a brief that Mike himself had just finished writing earlier.

'So tell me Mike, what do you think, is there anything you think that could connect these two incidents, they do seem quite different but at the same time I can see some similarities you know for example leaving the bodies to be found like that, I even got that impression with the body in the fire.'

'Jennifer Webb.'

'Yes, sorry Jennifer Webb, who ever did that could have easily destroyed her body before placing it in the fire unless he was disturbed in the process of course. And then of course in both cases there's the presence of a shoe being left at the scene, could be a coincidence of course but almost a calling card if you ask me and indicating that he or she is perhaps keeping some sort of a trophy cabinet. Twisted sick minds these people Mike.'

'Well, at the moment I'm undecided Ray, I can definitely see the possibility of them being linked of course.'

They had both arrived now in DCI Sheraton's office.

'Please take a seat Ray, there's something I want to show you which we received the other day,' said DCI Sheraton as he poured two cups of coffee.

DCI Sheraton then opened the brown folder on the top of his desk containing the two letters that had recently been sent to him. He took out just the one he had first received and handed it to DCI Pipe.

'This was addressed to myself Ray, see what you think.'

DCI Pipe sat down, read the letter, frowned to himself and sighed.

'Interesting, seen this sort of thing before and I'm sure you have Mike. Well, it could of course be from anyone who has read about both incidents in the local newspaper but nevertheless it could be from the offender, you can never tell. Has anyone else seen this?'

'Just myself and DS Hinckley, we've not released that information to anyone else.'

'Good, I think that's the right thing to do with this. Keep it on file for later. You never know with these things when they might become evidence. I'll tell you this though, all we just need now is an air accident and a buried body then we've got a full set Mike?'

'How do you mean?'

'The four elements of course Earth, Fire, Air and Water!'

'Good god, I'm hoping we are not looking at something like that, that's never crossed my mind, we've got enough on our plate with just these two.'

***

Blacon Police Station, Major Incident Room
Thursday, 11th *January 1968, 9.00am*

DCI Pipe and DCI Sheraton had agreed between them that their time together would best be served with DCI Pipe concentrating on the Operation Ulysses incident over at Blacon leaving DCI Sheraton to focus on the latest incident. They would however share any progress and ideas at the regular SIO review meetings. ACC Duckworth was happy with that situation for the time being.

The Operation Vanguard team were still desperately trying to identify the body that had been found at the disused boathouse back in December. Appeals and follow ups to the public for any information had now run dry. Although the House to House exercise had generated significant amounts of information there was now a huge backlog in writing this onto the cards in the manual indices. The vehicle sightings alone that had been spotted meant the officers were having to write seven cards for each vehicle to aid manually searching. No one had come forward to say their daughter or granddaughter had gone missing which was odd considering

Christmas had fallen just a couple of weeks after the girl's body had been found. The missing persons checks had also failed to produce any possible matches.

The Operation Vanguard team had now put out a further appeal to the public in trying to identify the girl that was found in the boatshed. DCI Sheraton was now in discussion with his incident team on their next moves when a phone call came into the incident room.

'Good morning, incident room DC Crowther speaking.'

'Good morning, is that the incident team that is investigating that boatshed murder?'

'It is yes, how can I help you?'

'Well, my name is Sarah Bellamy I'm not sure I should be contacting you but I haven't heard from one of my friends since before Christmas which I find rather odd. I saw your appeal and I really hope my friend Anne is safe and possibly still at her brothers. I know she was going away to stay with her brother down south and that was the last time we have heard from her. I've checked with my friends and they also haven't heard from her.'

'Okay, well let's start with a few details Sarah, firstly can I have your name and address?'

'Yes, it's Sarah Bellamy, 27 Wepre View, Deeside.'

'And your friend's name and address?'

'Her name is Anne Barlow, I'm afraid I don't know her address as she had recently moved into a bedsit somewhere in Shotton.'

'And when exactly did you last see her?'

'We were out together having a few drinks in Chester just before Christmas, it would be on Sunday, December 3rd.'

'And you haven't heard from her since?'

'Yes, that's right.'

'Not to worry Sarah, I'll pass these details on straight away and someone from the team will get back to you as soon as possible.'

DC Crowther replaced the receiver and dashed across to DS Hinckley who was searching again for possible missing persons within the area.

'Sarge, we have just had a call from someone called Sarah Bellamy, I think you should take a look at this.'

DS Hinckley scanned the note quickly.

'Right, thanks Nick, yes, this looks like it could be a possible breakthrough. Can you get back to talk to her urgently, find out where she lived before and presumably, she knows where her parents live, hopefully it's local as we need to get out to see them.'

'Will do Sarge.'

***

Friday, 12th January 1968, 9.30am

DC Crowther had wasted no time in getting back in touch with Sarah Bellamy and after some research he soon managed to find the address of Anne's parents John and Tricia Barlow who were living near Neston on the Wirral.

He was delighted to have a morning out of the office for a change as he drove down the A540 towards Heswall. It was now starting to rain hard almost sleeting and he was having difficulty spotting the sign for the turning into Quarry lane. At one point he thought he might have missed the turning and was about to turn back and then suddenly there it was, almost obscured by a road sign. He turned right down the narrow country lane and followed it for about a mile until he came to a set of large black wrought iron gates which had been left open.

As he followed the tree-lined private driveway, he still wasn't quite sure whether he was in the right place and then just after a bend in the drive there it was a magnificent manor house sitting proudly on an elevated position in approximately two acres of immaculate gardens in one of the Wirral's most prestigious areas. In the summer he imagined how the lawns would have been manicured without a grass out of place. The rain had suddenly got worse as he parked his mini clubman next to an immaculate white Rolls Royce Silver Shadow car at the side of a huge garage which presumably would have housed at least 4 or 5 cars.

Nick locked the car and walked briskly up the stone steps to the pillared entrance. He rang the doorbell and after a few minutes a dark-haired attractive lady in her late 40s came to the door.

'Good morning, is it Mrs Barlow?'

'Yes, it is how can I help?' she said with a concerned look.

Nick introduced himself and showed his warrant card briefly.

'I'm sorry to trouble you but I'm investigating a missing persons incident and I wonder if I could have a word with you Mrs Barlow, it shouldn't take too long.'

Nick decided he didn't want to go into specific details at this stage just in case Anne Barlow was safe and wasn't missing at all.

'Erm, yes please, come in out of the rain.'

Tricia Barlow led Nick into a huge impressive lounge area which overlooked a large internal swimming pool at the rear.

'So, how can I be of help Officer?'

'We received a phone call from a Miss Sarah Bellamy yesterday and...'

'I don't know anyone of that name,' she interjected shaking her head, 'should I know her?'

'Well, she is a close friend of your daughter Anne, she rang us to say she hasn't seen or heard from her since before Christmas.'

'Well, we haven't seen or heard from her either and to be honest we are not that bothered after the way she spoke to myself and my husband.'

'She stormed off and the last we heard is that she had found a bedsit somewhere on Deeside. She wrote to our son who lives in Basingstoke and he told us she seemed happy enough in her new place and was planning to visit him over Christmas. He did suggest however that we might like to write to her to make the peace. We were going on holiday when we received his letter and we have only just returned.'

'So your son gave you her new address?'

'Yes, I should have it here. Hang on a minute.'

Tricia Barlow went over to a fine antique satinwood writing desk and pulled out an envelope from the top right-hand drawer.

'This is it, yes, here's the address, I'll write it out for you.'

She passed the handwritten note to DC Crowther.

'Do you have a recent photograph of her Mrs Barlow?'

'Yes of course, you can take this one,' she replied handing him a framed photograph from the mantelpiece.

Nick took one look at the photograph, it certainly looked like the photo they had in the incident room.

'Thank you for your help Mrs Barlow, we'll get back to you once we have some news.'

'Yes, please do Officer, I'm really sorry we haven't reconciled our differences now, it was just a silly argument.'

'Well thanks for your time Mrs Barlow, I'll see myself out,' replied DC Crowther has he walked back to his car.

***

DC Crowther wasted no time in checking on the address that he'd been given by Tricia Barlow. He immediately contacted the landlord of the bedsit studio in Shotton. He confirmed that it had been rented to a Miss Anne Barlow at the beginning of November. She had taken it out initially on a six-month contract with an option to extend it when she had decided what to do. He had now also obtained a spare set of keys and arranged with a forensic officer to go with him to the bedsit.

The bedsit was easy to find on the main Queensferry road just before the railway bridge on the left-hand side. The officers knocked on the door first just in case Anne Barlow was at home after all. They had no reason to think otherwise. They knocked again but there was no answer, Nick placed the key in the lock and pushed open the door to piles of letters, newspapers and flyers on the floor.

The ground floor bedsit was smaller than he first thought but was kept extremely tidy. It had clearly been converted from what would have been originally a large three bedroomed terrace house. The furniture inside was sparse with just a sofa, book case and a glass coffee table. There was a small kitchenette at the far end which led into a partly tiled shower room and toilet. The forensic officer started immediately looking for any possible fingerprints that he could lift while DC Crowther looked for any documentation, letters, envelopes, diaries etc anything which might indicate if she had been planning to go away on holiday.

After about half an hour they had got what they needed and returned back to Blacon Police station.

Chapter 15

Tuesday, 16th January 1968, 10.30am

The call from forensics came through ten minutes after DCI Sheraton had returned to his office after visiting DCI Pipe at Blacon.

'Mike, it's Bob Coombes here, I have some news for you. Your victim is definitely confirmed as Anne Barlow. There's no doubt about it in my view, the fingerprints match.'

'Thanks Bob and I really appreciate your help.'

'No problem Mike, I don't envy you having to explain this to her parents. Anyway, good luck, let me know if we can help further.'

The DCI thanked the forensic team manager and replaced the receiver. He immediately asked everyone in the incident room to stop what they were working on and called them together to give them the news. Strangely they all seemed a bit puzzled and looked up from their desks which were now piled high with a mix of cards and paperwork.

'Gentlemen, the incident as from today takes on a new direction. We now have a fingerprint match of our victim at the boatshed. She is Anne Barlow from Shotton, Deeside. She was unemployed and living in a bedsit. Her parents haven't yet been told so please keep this within the incident room until we have delivered the press release. I will go over there today to break the sad news to her parents. Nick you have been over there once already and met Mrs Barlow, I'd like you to accompany me. Once we've done that, I'd like you all to glean as much information as you can get on Anne. We need to know everything about her, find out all her family, friends, boyfriends etc. In particular we need to know where she had been on the days leading up to that weekend. We want any sightings and in particular who was the last person to see her. I want those indexed as soon as possible.'

***

Tuesday, 16th January 1968, 11.45am

'Not an easy task this Nick. Do you know, no matter how many times you have to do it, it never gets any easier,' said DCI Sheraton as they headed towards Neston, 'this is the second time in the past two months I've had to do this.'

'I know what you mean sir, even the training can't really help you in this situation.'

Nick Crowther followed the country lane as before but was surprised this time to find the black wrought iron gates closed. He stepped out of the car and pressed the intercom.

'Not today thank you, can't you read the sign,' came the gruff voice back.

'It's Cheshire Police, we need to speak to you urgently,' replied DC Crowther who couldn't even see any sign.

Seconds later the gates slowly swung open and Nick Crowther followed the driveway up to the front of the house

'Bloody hell Nick, this is worth some money,' gasped the DCI, 'I hadn't realised she was from a well to do family.'

'Just wait till you see inside sir.'

They parked the unmarked police car next to the garage. There was no sign of the Rolls Royce which presumably was safely housed in the garage.

The two detectives walked across the gravel path and up the steps to the front door. This time an elderly silver haired gentleman, smartly dressed in beige trousers, brown oxford shoes and a blue open necked shirt with a paisley cravat was already waiting at the top of the steps.

'So how can I help you gentlemen?'

The DCI displayed his warrant card.

'Mr Barlow?' enquired the DCI.

'Yes, what seems to be the problem Officer?'

'I'm DCI Sheraton and this is DC Crowther, may we come in please?'

'Yes of course, come in.'

The two men were then shown into a large impressive dining room on the left which had a large oval shaped table and seating for at least a dozen people. At the far end of the dining room was a large seating area with two leather chesterfield sofas.

The DCI couldn't help noticing a large oil painting of a distinguished looking army officer above the marble mantelpiece.

'Please sit down and tell me how I can be of assistance?' said John Barlow thinking it was probably just something to do with crime prevention and security.

'Is Mrs Barlow also in?'

'She is Officer, but I'm afraid she is taking a bath at present and is unavailable.'

The DCI thought for a moment but decided he needed to break the news.

'Well Mr Barlow, I'm afraid I have some bad news. You may recall DC Crowther calling round here last week.'

'Yes, my wife told me that you had called,' replied John Barlow impatiently.

'Well, there is no easy way of telling you this but from that visit and further investigation I'm sorry to say that we have now identified the girl that was found in a disused boatshed in Chester. I'm so sorry Mr Barlow but we believe the girl was in fact your daughter Anne.'

The silence was deafening as John Barlow took the news in.

'Are you quite sure? I mean is there any chance it's not Anne, we understood she was away at her brothers.'

'No, I'm afraid not sir, she has been identified but we will need you to come over to formally identify her, we are so sorry to have to bring you this news but we will be in touch to arrange this.'

John Barlow was stunned and oddly his face showed no emotion whatsoever, then without warning he eventually broke the uneasy silence and stood up.

'Well, thank you for coming over gentlemen, appreciate you having to come over with this news. I'll inform Tricia immediately and I'll await your call to come over' sighed John Barlow.

They made their way to the front door and once again apologised to him in bringing the news.

The front door closed behind them and for a brief moment the DCI and DC stood there on the doorstep. The DCI thought for a moment in expressing his surprise in the manner how John Barlow dealt with the news almost as if he hadn't taken it in. Just as they had reached the car, they heard an almighty scream from an upstairs room.

Chapter 16

Cheshire Police HQ, Operation Vanguard Incident Room –
Monday, 22nd January 1968, 10.30am

DCI Pipe and DCI Sheraton had decided to switch a few of the officers between incident rooms. One of those transfers was a switch involving PC Walker moving to Operation Ulysses in return for DC Johnson who moved to Operation Vanguard.

The Vanguard incident room had fallen way behind with the indexing and a serious backlog had now built up hence Peter Johnson being transferred to help speed things up. The move suited Peter who lived about a mile from HQ in Handbridge.

He had been given the documents, diaries and the address book that had been found at Anne Barlow's bedsit to index.

As he sat down writing the nominal cards in the card index, he couldn't help noticing a reference to the name Jennifer Webb who he was surprised to find was also a friend of Anne Barlow's. He thought at first it must be a coincidence and possibly someone with the same name. He double checked it, said nothing and dashed down the corridor to see the DCI.

'Are you quite sure?' said the DCI, 'I mean does the address match?'

'Yes, I've checked it. I couldn't believe it.'

Suddenly the DCI realised they did have a linked incident after all.

***

Friday, 16th February 1968

Both the Blacon and Chester incident rooms were now working at full capacity and totally resourced. With both bodies now formally identified the investigation teams were working flat out to try and identify the offender. DCI Sheraton now firmly held the belief it was the work of one man but DCI Pipe was still open minded on the subject. The decision had been taken to run both operations from Blacon and Chester which was not ideal under the circumstances but at least the incident rooms were in constant touch with each other. With no Major Incident computer system available it was inevitable that duplication of actions and recording on cards would take place. To try and overcome this DCI Sheraton had insisted that any actions required to interview witnesses should at least be handled by the Chester incident room.

***

Cheshire Police HQ, Office of ACC Crime
Tuesday, 19th March 1968, 10.30am

The ACC had called in DCI Sheraton and DCI Pipe to cover the investigation progress of both incidents but this was no ordinary progress meeting both DCI's knew deep down this could result in the force's decision to close the incidents as unsolved.

'So Mike, time is moving on, are we any nearer in finding our offender on the Anne Barlow case? said the ACC as he opened the meeting.

'Well sir, after following all our leads we do have a couple of possible suspects. I am not convinced that the owner of the boatshed Alfred Dixon had nothing to do with it. The timing of his immediate departure on that Saturday afternoon means he could very well have committed this crime early on that very morning, long before anyone would have been up and about on that riverbank. He has been known to frequent some of the pubs and clubs late at night and he has been cautioned before over an assault on one of his female staff. This was several years ago and it was only the woman who changed her story that prevented him from being charged. It was his wife who gave him his alibi of course for his movements on that Saturday. We also checked on when this so-called holiday of his was booked. He booked it last minute on the Saturday morning!'

'What did the forensic officers come up with?' enquired the ACC as he continued to scribble his notes.

'They have lifted a number of fingerprints but of course as it was his boatshed you would expect his to turn up.'

'She was found naked, wasn't she, did we ever find the clothing?'

'No sir.'

'You mentioned a couple of suspects Mike?'

'Yes sir, you might recall a sighting of a strange vehicle and a couple arguing not far from the location. We never did find the vehicle nor the couple. All we do know is that it was a grey Austin Cambridge A55 saloon, we don't have a registration.'

'What vehicle does Alfred Dixon own?'

'That's a red Vauxhall estate.

'So all in all, we haven't got any further,' sighed the ACC, 'Ray, tell me how have you got on?'

'Well sir, as you know we consider that both these incidents are linked after discovering that both victims were well known to each other. This might seem a coincidence but we believe we are looking for the same offender.'

'And are there any links to your suspects?'

'None, we cannot find any link to Alfred Dixon, as far as we can ascertain he didn't know either girl.'

'We have our doubts on Kenneth Smith, even if he did visit his so-called girlfriend Sheila Gilderson, he could have easily had time to get into Chester City Centre and meet Jennifer Webb earlier that night. We checked the tyre marks in the surrounding lanes close to where the body was found and matched them to Kenneth Smith's vehicle but of course he drove around the place regularly.'

'So what about her boss Norman Arrowsmith?'

'Again, he has stayed on our radar throughout this investigation. He certainly had the opportunity and we know from talking to people who know him he had a bit of a thing about Jennifer Webb. I think it's unlikely however that he did it but he certainly knows how to draw attention to himself,' smiled the DCI.

'Next, we have Bill Newton the taxi driver. He could well have been the last person to see Jennifer alive. We never did find the youth from Buckley he mentioned but of course we didn't have a lot to go on. Several people from Buckley come into Chester city centre on a weekend. His story about having a brew afterwards at the taxi office didn't stack up but maybe that was his memory playing tricks.'

'And then we come to Nigel Simpson, Jennifer's boss who worked with her in the night club and probably was one of the last people to see her alive. Again, through talking to her fellow colleagues in work we know Nigel quite fancied her, he'd even remarked to one of them that he was going to ask her out. We also checked out his vehicle which had been seen parking at her block of flats not long after she had been murdered. He denied he'd been to her flat. It's also likely that he knew Anne Barlow her friend who had been known to come to the club and that sir is where we are currently with the investigation.'

The ACC thought for a while before responding.

'Fascinating gentlemen,' said the ACC, 'I for one have really appreciated the hard work you have both put in on these investigations but I'm afraid we appear no nearer to finding our offender or should I say offenders. I've been thinking carefully about how much longer we can continue with these investigations and with pressure from above I'm afraid we've had to make the decision that we have no option but to close the incidents and mark them as unsolved at this stage.

Naturally if further information comes to hand, we will re-open the cases.'

'DCI Pipe I'd also like to personally thank you for your assistance on this and I know for a fact Mike here has also appreciated your help. I wish you well on your return to the Met and thanks again for your efforts.'

'Thank you, sir,' said DCI Pipe,' it's been a pleasure working with your force I'm just sorry we didn't get an outcome and can I just say it's been an absolute pleasure working with DCI Sheraton.'

DCI Pipe closed his folder, shook hands with both officers and left the office.

'I wonder if I may have a word with you sir,' said DCI Sheraton as he reached for a letter in his jacket pocket.

Part 2

Chapter 17

Raven's Clough, Cheshire
Wednesday, 14th February 2001

On a beautiful sunny, cold but almost spring like morning a party of seventeen walkers from the Congleton ramblers met for their weekly walk. They were a hardy bunch and nothing would deter them from their weekly walk. They were mostly retired and would be out in most weathers every week on a Wednesday morning without fail. Today was a special walk of eight miles culminating in a specially arranged Valentine's Day lunch at a local hostelry. They met as arranged at 10.00am promptly at the public car park at Timbersbrook on Weathercock Lane. Once suitably booted and equipped they followed the dirt track climbing steadily up through the trees eventually reaching the Cloud summit. The view from the top of the hill on this particular day across the Cheshire plain was stunning with not a cloud in the sky and the walkers decided to have a break, it was just too good to move on. They decided to stop for a short coffee break accompanied by a selection of valentine day chocolates. The group took their break sheltering from the cold wind behind rocks just below the summit.

The walkers suitably refreshed, then regrouped and continued onwards down the footpath to Red Lane before joining the South Staffordshire and Gritstone trail. This was a walk they had done several times before. It was just before they had got to Raven's Clough when one of their party Jim Smithson a retired police custody sergeant from the Cheshire force was curious at the sight of smoke coming from the chimney of an old disused stone-built hut which was about 400 metres from the footpath. They'd walked past the small hut several times in the past and in fact it had become a bit of a landmark on their previous walks but they had never seen it occupied before.

'I'll catch you up later everyone, there's something not quite right here,' shouted Jim to the party leader, 'I'm just going to check this out, it does seem a bit odd.'

'It's probably a local farmer or just a tramp living in there Jim, I wouldn't worry too much about it!' exclaimed one of the group.

'You are probably right but nevertheless it's worth taking a look at,' shouted Jim who had already started wandering off in that direction.

'Once a copper always a copper, we'll wait for you by the farm,' retorted Gordon the walking group leader as the group continued on down towards the farmhouse in the valley below.

Jim went over to the hut which presumably had been used as some form of shelter for farmers and even possibly sheep several years ago. He thought about knocking to see if anyone was in there, he peered through the small dusty window but couldn't see anyone. To his surprise a large rock had been placed in front of the door. He carefully rolled the rock to one side and lifted the rusty metal latch. The wooden door to his surprise was unlocked and opened with surprisingly relative ease. The first thing though that hit him was the foul aroma which almost took his breath away. The place was filthy and smelt of a strange mix of manure, sour milk and raw sewage. As he entered the hut, he could see the embers of a small fire burning in an old-fashioned brick hearth. The fire was almost out but just enough to generate a few wisps of smoke. A few logs were piled in one corner and hanging up on a rusty nail which had been banged into one of the old beams was an old green wax jacket. On the table in front of him he could see a discarded cider bottle and the remains of hand rolled cigarettes which had been stubbed out into a rusty old Golden Virginia tobacco tin. He initially thought there must be a tramp taking shelter living there and he was about to leave when he noticed a large bundle of what looked like rags on the concrete floor. He slowly approached the bundle, was about to turn it over and it was then that he saw the huge pool of blood which had been oozing out from under the rags. He didn't dare disturb it and dashed out, wasting no time in reaching for his mobile phone and calling 999.

***

The Command and Control room at Chester Police HQ had been as busy ever when the call came through and the dispatchers wasted no time in getting Congleton CID and the supporting officers out to the incident location, which was easier said than done to what was indeed a remote location at the south eastern end of the force area. A mile further on and the incident could well have been investigated by Staffordshire or for that matter even Derbyshire Police.

Although not far from the town it also wasn't quite obvious as to how to best reach the rural scene. DCI Kevin Maxfield accompanied by DS Hopkins arrived at the scene having managed to park their silver Vauxhall Omega estate in the lane at the end of the fields just below the Cloud hill. Four uniformed officers were also immediately despatched to the area to conduct house to house enquiries in the immediate area. The Scenes of Crime officer and the pathologist Dr Frank James had already arrived just before them and were already examining the body inside the hut. The weather had also changed from the promise of a bright wintry day and flecks of driving snow had now appeared this time coming from an easterly direction.

'I wouldn't mind betting Buxton is getting it at present,' remarked DS Hopkins pointing to the dark grey skies as they made their way down the old bridleway.

The DCI nodded in agreement.

As the two CID officers arrived in the field, they could see that the area around the hut had already been cordoned off.

Two uniformed officers and a somewhat familiar looking man wearing walking boots, waterproofs, a trekking pole and a rucksack stood at the entrance to the hut.

'I know you from somewhere, don't I?' said the DCI to Jim Smithson who was now busy chatting to one of the officers.

'You should do Kevin, the name is Jim Smithson. I was the custody sergeant over at the Middlewich nick. I've processed quite a few of your arrests in the past I can tell you.

I'm now retired of course, we were out walking and noticed the smoke, then discovered this.'

'Ah yes, Sergeant Smithson,' said the DCI as he shook hands, 'I thought I knew your face. It's good to see you again. It's been quite a long time. Retired eh, can't be bad. Yes, I gather it was yourself who called the control room. Well spotted Jim.'

'To be honest it was pure curiosity really, it could have been someone dossing here for all I know. I knew something was wrong when I saw the wisps of smoke coming from the building. We've walked this path loads of times and never seen anything like this before.'

'Bet you thought there had been a new pope announcement?'

'Pardon,' said Jim looking somewhat puzzled.

'Nothing, just my little joke. Nevertheless, thank you Jim for calling us. Anyway, it's good to see you again despite the circumstances, now if you'll excuse me, I really must get on and see what we have in here. Will probably see you later on to go through your statement with you.'

The DCI and DS donned their protective suits and paper slipover shoes. As they entered the hut the pathologist was already kneeling down besides the girl's body and was in the process of instructing a young Scenes of Crime officer to take a number of various photographs of the body from differing angles.

'Morning both. Good god Frank you are on the ball, you beat me to it this time, so what have we got here?'

'Good morning Kevin, yes, I was working in Congleton this morning as it happened so it didn't take me more than five minutes once I got the call on my mobile to get over here. I know the area quite well anyway. I do a bit of clay pigeon shooting over this way. Anyway, it's a young girl, I'd say she's probably no more than eighteen years of age, she's been struck from the back of the head by a hammer or something similar, will be able to give you more when we get her body back to the mortuary. There are some scratch marks on her arms and bruising to the wrists suggesting that some form of struggle has taken place but apart from that I can't really tell you much more at this stage. I can't really give you the time of death at present although I'd say she's been dead for a good eight hours or so possibly earlier. I guess the embers still burning in the fire leads us to thinking it was probably yesterday. I should have a clearer idea after I've performed the autopsy.'

The DCI being careful not to touch anything looked around the hut which was sparsely furnished. 'So we have no documents, handbag etc or anything found here, nothing on her I don't suppose?'

'Nothing sir, presumably who ever has done this didn't want to her to be identified easily. Although we do have this sir,' interjected the SOCO, 'she was wearing this charm bracelet on her right wrist. I can't quite make the engraving out it looks like the letters CW, what looks like a heart shape and the letter A although it could be a 4. It's a pretty bad engraving to be honest, I think someone might have scratched it on themselves.'

The DCI muttered something and took a closer look at it without handling the bracelet.

'Yes, I see what you mean, well bag it up anyway.'

At this point the pathologist turned the body over and it was the first time they could actually see the girls face which was heavily bruised. DCI Maxfield shook his head and frowned at the sight before him, he'd seen it all before of course over the years but it still came as a bit of a shock.

'Do you recognise her at all Kevin, does she seem at all familiar to you?' asked Frank James.

The DCI shook his head, 'Can't say I've seen her before. Well, I've been based around here for the past ten years Frank and I certainly don't recognise her but it's quite possible of course she's not from this area anyway!' exclaimed the DCI looking for some sort of confirmation from his sergeant.

DS Hopkins shook his head in agreement. The SOCO continued to carefully move around them quietly taking photographs guided only by the pathologist.

'Okay Hopkins, there is really not much more we can do here now. Let's leave these gentlemen to get on with their work, it's back to the station to organise the incident room and I'd say by the look of that black cloud towards Mow Cop over there we are in for a bit of a snow storm so best get a move on. Thanks again Frank, I shall look forward to your report, keep me posted. We've got an incident room to setup.'

***

DCI Maxfield was taken by complete surprise as he entered the Congleton Police Station just thirty minutes after leaving the scene. As soon as he had entered the CID office, he was handed a small bundle of officer reports which were still handwritten and as yet awaiting typing up from the initial house to house enquiries.

'I thought you might like to take a quick look at these, sir, before they go in for typing, there was only a couple of farm cottages so we took the opportunity,' said the uniformed officer.

'Blimey that was quick. Yes, thanks I'll hand them back to typing as soon as I've had a chance to read them.'

With only a few properties such as farm cottages in the area the officers had been quick off the mark knocking at the doors of each house and asking residents if they had seen or heard anything suspicious over the weekend. The residents hadn't really seen or heard anything out of the normal.

The DCI took a quick glance through each one of them and made a few mental notes before handing them back.

He was even more surprised when he entered the incident room and he'd half expected the IT support guys to still be working on cabling and installing software however the Holmes incident room was now fully set up and resourced in readiness. Terminals and printers were now all configured, set up and awaiting the indexing of the incident data which was about to appear from the enquiry teams. Even the major incident team members were also seated, ready, eager and waiting, keyboards and mice at the ready.

The DCI thought to himself, *He'd never even seen it setup so quickly, DS Sharon Hayes had done a superb job organising it all and in such a short time.*

'Good grief Sharon, we'd still be looking for the index cards in the store room on the old system by now,' he laughed, 'well done everyone, a good start, let's hope it's an omen in solving this one pretty quickly.'

'What's he mean by cards?' whispered one of the trainee indexers who was just logging onto his terminal on the Holmes computer system.

The DCI smiled but ignored the comment by one of the new police probationary officers who had been drafted in to assist with the indexing of the data.

'Welcome to the 21st century boss. With all the practice and exercise training we get, we have it down to a fine art now,' replied DS Hayes as she started to prepare the wall boards which would be used to display the various photographic, geographic and link charts.

'I can see that. Now listen up everyone. This is the position right now this is what have we got so far, let's just have a swift recap on what we know. A young girl's body probably eighteen to twenty years of age has been found badly beaten up in a sheep farmer's disused hut in a remote field just out of town not far from the Timbersbrook area. We also have two separate sightings of a youth running away from that area on Middle Lane yesterday afternoon 13th February in the direction of Buglawton. The forensic officer has already told me there are a number of prints and blood stains that he's found on the doorframe and on the table in particular. We should also get post mortem and forensic reports back any time. I've had a quick glance at the early house to house reports which mention a youth that was seen running away from the area on Tuesday. Now I'm keen to follow up on that young man who was seen legging it in the direction of the town centre, it may have nothing to do with it but we can't discount it at this stage. We also have a report from a local farmer who says he saw a young couple arguing on Tunstall Road near Timbersbrook which leads to the public footpath in the area. We don't have an approximate time of death but it's quite feasible it could have been sometime yesterday afternoon, we will know more when the pathologist gives us his full report. We don't have any identity of the girl, although she was left fully clothed, there was nothing left at the scene, no purse, handbag, belongings etc nothing apart from a bracelet so we are going to have to rely on an appeal on missing persons. We will make an appeal at the press conference which has been arranged for tomorrow morning. We cannot unfortunately show her face as she was so badly beaten. So on with it everyone unless there are any questions?'

DS Hayes raised her hand. 'You mention the sightings sir, presumably the youth was running into town. Are there any CCTV cameras in that area which might be of help here?'

'Well, there are a couple Sharon, but to be honest the quality of image probably won't provide us with much to go on. But it's worth taking a look anyway.'

'Okay, if there are no more questions I shall be in my office if you need me.'

***

Congleton Police Station
Thursday, 15th February 2001

DCI Maxfield and the ACC Crime took their respected places at the Press conference which was being held in a small conference room in Congleton Police Station. Reporters from local newspapers and cameras from the BBC managed to cram into the small space.

The DCI stood up under the watchful eye of the ACC and opened the press briefing.

'Good morning. I am sorry to have to tell you that yesterday morning a girl's body was found at a disused hut at Ravens Clough not far from here near Timbersbrook. We are appealing for any witnesses to come forward who may have seen anything suspicious in that area of the town on Tuesday this week.

We are currently trying to identify the victim who is white, she is possibly aged between eighteen and twenty years, of slim build, with blonde short cropped hair and was wearing blue jeans, Nike trainers, a maroon top and a parka style coat. If anyone recognises the description of the victim and has any information, then please get in touch. Also, if anyone recognises this bracelet which was found near the scene, we would ask you to please contact the incident room at Congleton Police station as soon as possible.'

***

Congleton Chronicle, Cheshire
Thursday, 22nd February 2001

A murder investigation has been launched after finding a woman's body last week on Wednesday morning 14th February in a disused hut at Ravens Clough, near Timbersbrook according to the Cheshire Constabulary. The identity of the deceased is yet to be formally established.

Detectives believe that the unidentified victim was brutally murdered and left in the hut around the 13th February. The victim is believed to have been between 18 and 21 according to the senior investigating officer Detective

Chief Inspector Kevin Maxfield at Cheshire CID who is leading the investigation.

The body was actually found by a retired police officer – Mr Jim Smithson who was out walking with Congleton Ramblers on the Wednesday morning.

Officers are particularly keen to trace a youth that was seen running from the area in the direction of the town on the Tuesday afternoon.

Anyone with any information is asked to please contact the incident room at Congleton Police station.

***

Travellers Inn, Same Day, 1.00pm

Sally Bateman was busy washing and drying the pint glasses at the Travellers Inn near Congleton when the BBC North West lunchtime news came on showing an appeal by Cheshire Police and in particular displaying a photo of the bracelet that was found on the body at Ravens Clough.

'Reg, Reg I've seen that before,' she shouted to her husband who was working down in the cellar, 'there was a girl in here standing by the bar a couple of weeks ago showing it off to her boyfriend, I can remember them arguing.'

Reg suddenly appeared from the cellar door.

'What's all the fuss woman? Have you broken something again?'

'No, no there was an appeal on the telly for anyone who has seen a particular bracelet,' she said pointing at the telly which had now moved onto a completely different news story,

'She'd just bought it apparently with his money and he didn't seem best pleased.'

'Who had?'

'This girl who has been found murdered apparently. I can remember the both of them they stood here for a while at the bar arguing with each other for ages. She even dangled it in front of him almost taunting him like she'd spent his hard-earned money on herself.'

'Well, you'd best get onto the Police straight away.'

'I will, I will. Can you look after the bar while I'm gone? I'll get my coat on and get down there now.'

***

Cheshire Police HQ, ACC Crime's Office

DCI Maxfield had decided that he had no option but to make the hour-long trip over to force HQ.

The Holmes incident room was now working flat out. DS Hayes was running the incident as the office manager and she was well organised. But a week further on and still no one had come forward to ask about their daughter, granddaughter, sister or friend. All mispers in the area had been checked out with no matches. Officers were naturally keen to try and identify the youth who had been seen running into town on the Tuesday before the body was found.

DCI Maxfield took the lift to the senior command suite and entered the ACC's PA office.

'Oh, good afternoon Kevin,' said Beryl, 'he's ready to see you and told me to tell you to go straight in.'

'Great thanks Beryl.'

Ian Mossley the ACC Crime had only been in post a few months and had worked with Kevin Maxfield on a number of cases over the past ten years before his promotion from Chief Superintendent. Kevin and Ian had worked well together in the past and the ACC had responded very quickly to Kevin's request for an urgent meeting.

'Good afternoon sir, thanks for arranging the meeting at such short notice.'

'Not at all, Kevin. It gives us the opportunity to catch up with how you are progressing with this latest incident. I assume you have everything you need, you've got enough trained Holmes staff?'

'Well, yes sir, the Holmes system is performing well and we have a great investigation team, the indexers are on top of everything. No serious backlogs to tell you about. No complaints there at all sir.'

'I can hear a but coming?'

'Well, it's not quite a but sir. I want to run a mass DNA screening and I need to get authority from yourself to go ahead.'

'Good grief, is there any alternative, these things cost a fortune you know?'

'Well, the alternative sir is that we plough on hoping to get a breakthrough on a sighting for example. We still don't have an identity of our victim and to be honest I can't see that changing in the near future. What we do have is a number of sightings of a youth running away from the area the day before. I think this youth holds the key to our investigation, it's just a guess but I think he was the girl's boyfriend. We find him and I believe we are nearer to closing the case.'

'Right, well I admire your confidence Kevin. How many youths are we looking at in taking part in this screening?'

'Well, I think we can restrict it on an age range sir. My gut feel is about 300 between 18 and 21, living in the Congleton area, we might have to widen the screening of course if we get a negative response.'

'Bloody hell, I can't make a decision like that on my own. This is quite a costly process we are talking about but leave it with me and I'll get straight back to you.'

'Thank you, sir.'

***

Congleton Police Station Front Desk
Thursday, 22nd February 2001, 2.30pm

'So can you describe this couple madam?'

'Yes, it was about three weeks ago Officer, she had blonde hair cropped short I think, I'd say she was about 5'2", attractive girl aged about 19 years but there was something about her which was wrong.'

'How do you mean?'

'Well, she had a bit of an edge to her if you ask me, a chip on her shoulder as if the world owed her living. She treated her boyfriend like dirt. I was amazed he put up with her to be honest.'

'Can you describe what she was wearing?'

'Yes, I think she had black jeans and a sort of maroon top probably more purple than maroon. Pretty casually dressed really but quite smart, lots of makeup.'

'And her boyfriend, can you describe him?'

'Oh, he looked slightly older than her but probably 19 or no more than 20 years of age. He looked as though he hadn't got two pennies to rub together. I felt a bit sorry for him actually. He would be about 5'4" I guess, dark short hair, unshaven I think. Looked as though he could do with a good bath. He was scruffy, he had a tatty pair of jeans and a tee shirt, trainers oh that's it he was wearing a black AC/DC shirt.'

'So this bracelet, can you describe it?'

'Yes, it was silver and it had a number of charms on it. I know one was a silver elephant and I can remember a silver imp like charm, pixie sort of thing. At one time she left it on the bar whilst she was arguing with him that's when I saw it.'

'So can you recall them coming in your pub before?'

'Yes, they had been in a couple of times, they never really spoke to any of the locals. I think they were new to the area but they seemed to live locally. At a guess I'd say they had southern accents, not your local accents, pretty sure they weren't from around here.'

'Did you manage to catch either of their names at all?'

'I didn't catch the lad's name but I think he called her Emma or it might have been Amy, but I might be wrong, I could have misheard it.'

'Well, thanks Mrs Bateman, that's been most helpful, we may need to contact you later if that's okay.'

'Yes, that's fine Officer, you know where we are, we serve a cracking pint!'

***

DCI Maxfield was on his way back from Chester and had almost reached Congleton when his mobile rang. He switched on the hands free and was surprised to hear the voice of the ACC Crime.

'Hi Kevin, I thought you would want to know as soon as possible, the chief has given you permission to run that DNA screening on the basis of no more than 300 samples.'

'That's fantastic news, thanks sir I'll start making the necessary arrangements.'

'I didn't tell the chief we might have to widen the sample area, let's just hope this brings in the result we are after.'

'Thanks sir, I really appreciate your help with this one. Will keep you posted.'

DCI Maxfield closed the call and whooped with joy as he sped back into Congleton. Some ten minutes later he'd parked up in the station yard and was back in the incident room.

'Have I missed anything Sharon, while I've been out?'

'Well, we have received an interesting visit at the front desk, not long ago. The lady who runs the Travellers pub down the road called and she thinks the girl and her boyfriend had been rowing there. She recognised the bracelet. She's given us a decent description of the lad. She thinks they are living local.'

'Did she mention his age?'

'She said he was about 19 or 20.'

'That's it then, I've just had permission from the chief to do a DNA mass screening, can you get it organised. I think we might have just turned a corner!'

Chapter 18

Congleton Chronicle, Cheshire
Thursday, 8th March 2001

DNA testing of some 300 young men will start today in an attempt to find the killer of the girl who was found murdered and left in a disused hut at Ravens Clough near Congleton last month. The girl who has not yet been identified is believed to have been arguing with her boyfriend just prior to her murder.

A team of officers from Cheshire Police are to call on all young men aged between 18 and 21 living in Congleton and will collect samples which will be compared with the blood samples which were discovered at the scene.

The police will take mouth swabs from males aged 18 to 21 in order to obtain a DNA profile.

***

Congleton Police Station, Incident Room
Monday, 26th March 2001

It had been almost three weeks since the force had started carrying out the mass DNA screening with 297 young men now taking part. At first a small number of them refused to co-operate but when it was explained to them that they would then have to be interviewed as part of the incident if they didn't take part, they soon changed their minds.

DCI Maxfield and his team were waiting patiently for the results which they knew could take some time. They were reviewing the case in the incident room when the DCI received the phone call from the DNA analysis team, the phone call that he had been waiting for.

'Good morning Kevin, it's Dr Jim Reed we've got some interesting news for you.'

The DCI couldn't believe his ears.

'Okay Jim, hit me with it, what have you found?'

'We have a match on the sample batch record number 134, there is no doubt about it.'

'Wonderful news, are you sure?'

The DCI didn't know why he'd even asked that, he was almost trying to get the words back in his mouth on querying whether they were sure or not.

'Yes, positive Kevin.'

'Great, we'll follow that up straight away but just hang on a second Jim.'

The DCI dropped the phone and waved over for DS Hayes to bring the screening list over. He quickly scanned down the list of names for record number 134 and found a nineteen-year-old named Cameron Wilkinson. The first thing that jumped out at him however was his initials CW, surely it had to be him.

The DCI picked up the phone again, 'That's wonderful Jim, we can move straight away on that.'

'Actually, Kevin there is more?'

'How do you mean there's more?'

'Well, when we ran the matching process, we don't just match on one case from the DNA database we match against any other outstanding cases which of course some may have been closed a while ago as unsolved incidents.'

'Right, and?'

'Well, from that screening process we have another match, a completely separate match, batch record number 186 matches against two other linked cases. Cold cases in fact from the late 1960s which are still tagged as unsolved.'

'Well, how can that be, the sample donors weren't even born then?'

'Yes, but it's familial DNA you see, there must be a link from one of these donors through generations of his family.'

The DCI couldn't believe what he was hearing.

'Right, look can you send me your report as soon as possible and we'll follow these up.'

'You've done a great job, thanks Jim.'

The DCI wasted no time in looking back down the list for batch record number 186 and that's when he sat down in shock.

He thought to himself, *Surely, it can't be.*

Chapter 19

Congleton Police Station –
Monday, 26th March 2001, 5pm

DCI Maxfield immediately called the landlord to find out the list of tenant's names for the address that Cameron Wilkinson had given when providing his sample.

DS Hayes and a uniformed officer in the meantime wasted no time in getting over to Cameron Wilkinson's flat which was one of four in a converted terraced house on the main Buxton Road not far out of the town centre. The brick-built house was badly run down and looked as though it was well beyond repair and in need of demolition. The windows and doors were rotten to the core. One of the previous residents had also tried to patch up one of the windows with a sheet of plywood which was now flapping wildly in the breeze. It looked more like a typical squatter's house than a residential flat.

'Give him a couple of minutes to answer the door,' said the DS and if he doesn't answer, then we'll take the door down.

'It won't take much,' laughed the burly uniformed officer, 'If I give it one good knock, I reckon it'll probably fall down of its own accord.'

Minutes later a sleepy eyed, bare footed Cameron Wilkinson dressed in dirty denim jeans and a dark grey tee shirt came to the door.

'Cameron Wilkinson?' asked DS Hayes politely.

'Yes, what's the problem?'

'I'm DS Hayes and we'd like you to come down to the police station where we need to ask you a few questions.'

'I'm afraid it's not really convenient at the moment. I've not long been home from work and I need to get some sleep. Can I come down later?'

'Sorry son, get your shoes on, there'll be time for a sleep afterwards,' said DS Hayes thinking, *There's a nice little cell at the station where you'll have plenty of time for a sleep.*

DS Hayes read him his rights and Cameron Wilkinson muttered something incomprehensible in return. He then slipped on a pair of old grubby trainers, grabbed his door keys and climbed into the back of the waiting police car.

Five minutes later he was sat in interview room 1.

'My name is DCI Maxfield and my role today is to interview you in relation to the offence(s) that you've been arrested on suspicion for. I will also be making notes during the interview purely for my reference. Also present is DS Wood and Mr James Carlisle the duty solicitor. Firstly, can you give me your full name please.'

'Cameron Wilkinson.'

'And your date of birth?'

'30th March 1981'

'For the benefit of the tape I'm now showing the defendant a photograph. Cameron do you recognise this girl?'

Cameron winced and shifted uneasily when he saw the photograph. Suddenly his face lost all colour and he looked as though he was going to be sick as he looked away towards the door. But then to the officer's surprise, Cameron suddenly placed his head in his hands and started sobbing uncontrollably.

'Well, Cameron, I shall ask you again, do you recognise this girl in the photograph?'

Cameron shrugged. 'No comment.'

'Is this your girlfriend Amy Graham?'

'No comment.'

'Were you in a relationship with Amy Graham.'

'No comment.'

'Is there anything you wish to tell us?'

'No nothing.'

'C'mon son, we know you did this. We have your fingerprints and your DNA placing you at the scene. It's not going to do you any good keeping this lot bottled up. In fact, it will help you feel much better if you get it off your chest.'

Cameron Wilkinson hesitated and for the first time lifted his head up and wiped the tears away.

He said slowly, 'Yes, yes, she was my girlfriend but she had abused me.'

'So you did have a relationship with Amy Graham?'

'Yes sir, she was my girlfriend,' he blurted out, 'it wasn't supposed to be like this, we loved each other very much.'

'So tell me about this relationship Cameron.'

'Well, at first, we had a great relationship, we were so much in love but it all went very sour. I'll never forget the moment that she first started abusing me. Initially it was by name calling, I could put up with that but this developed into her even scalding me by pouring boiling water over me. We'd recently moved up to the Congleton area from down south and moved into a nice little flat in Buglawton. We were happy there at first. We knew no one up here but I soon found friends through work. At first things seemed alright between us but gradually she became angry with me for some odd reason when just for example I wanted to go out with my workmates to the football or for a mid-week game of snooker. My mates told me they wouldn't put up with it. In the end I'd had enough of it and decided to ignore her one day. I went out with my mates, when I came back, she'd already boiled the kettle and threw it all over me when I arrived back home at the flat. The pain was like nothing I'd ever experienced before and I begged her to stop, she laughed and seemed to enjoy it. I told them in Macclesfield A&E that it had been an accident but I'm sure they didn't believe me.

She became jealous of the friends I had but then she tried to isolate me from all my friends and family. Often when they called, she would tell them I was at work when I wasn't. I was at home all the time. I would arrive home from work tired and hungry and she would have eaten her own meal but refused to make anything for me. I know my mates had kept asking me why on earth I was still living with her but it was me who was paying the rent, she didn't work at all and most days she just stayed in bed. She never cleaned the place, I had to do that when I arrived home. She had no friends or family to speak of and wanted nothing whatsoever to do with any of mine.

We'd been together for just over a year. In the end it became so unbearable that I was really scared of her. Amy and I were seventeen when we first met at a college down in Bedfordshire, we were just good friends at first and then we fell in love. All that changed when we came up here to live. We had constant rows in the flat and one day our neighbour even called the police when they heard her shouting abuse at me. When they came and knocked at the door, I made excuses for her and actually lied to them. I played the whole thing down saying we were just fooling around. We moved out of the flat into this place, I was struggling to make ends meet.

The strange thing is, do you know I still love her as some days she would switch back into that lovely person that I first met in college. We had some good times together Amy and I, laughing and joking. I had a day off work and we decided to go for a walk on that Tuesday morning. It was then that she started going on at me again, all the time throughout the walk, nagging, constant nagging. Telling me I was worthless and that I needed to find another job.

It had started to snow quite heavily and we decided to take shelter in that hut. I managed to find a few sticks and lit a fire to keep warm. Someone had left a few logs so we piled those on. She kept saying I would never make anything of myself and I decided to just leave her there. I started walking back and she came after me. We had a furious row and she just wouldn't stop until in the end I snapped. I waited for the right moment and when she wasn't looking, I grabbed a rock and smashed her over the head with it. I don't regret it, she drove me to it. Even when she was out cold, she still seemed to be laughing at me so I hit her again and again. The anger was seething in me. I thought about just leaving her there on the moorland but I dragged her back into that hut. In a strange way it was a weight off my shoulders, suddenly I felt enormous relief.'

'And where did you go then?'

'I went back into the Congleton town centre. I needed a drink, I can't remember the name of the pub, it's not often I come into the town, most of my money goes to her. It was the pub immediately across the road from the town hall. I had a few pints in there and then walked home.'

'That would probably be the White Lion. So did you speak to anybody in the pub?'

'No, I didn't recognise anyone in there.'

'So what time was that?'

'I'd say it would be about 4 o'clock.'

'So at what time did you leave the pub?'

'I don't remember.'

'And where did you go afterwards?'

'I went straight home to the flat.'

'And then…'

'I bundled all her belongings, clothes and everything, shoved them into five bin bags and took them straight to the tip on the Wednesday morning. I just wanted rid of all memories of her.'

DCI Maxfield had decided he had heard enough.

'Cameron Wilkinson, I am arresting you for the murder of Amy Graham. You do not have to say anything. But, it may harm your defence if you do not mention when questioned something which you later rely on in court. Anything you do say may be given in evidence.'

***

DCI Maxfield and DS Wood made their way across the corridor into the incident room and closed the door shut behind them. There was an eerie hush somehow as the investigation team were waiting with baited breath on the outcome of the interview. The DCI decided to put on a sad expression as he felt all those around him were watching his facial expression.

'We've got him!' he exclaimed, 'He's confessed!'

The cheers went around the room and from somewhere at the back of the room almost immediately out came a bottle of something fizzy followed by a tray of plastic cups.

'The work is not yet over everybody, there is a lot to do but well done everyone. I'm just off to ring the ACC about another matter. DS Wood can you prepare the relevant MG forms for the CPS.'

'Yes of course sir.'

DCI Maxfield returned to his office and picked up the phone.

'Hello sir, I just want you know that Cameron Wilkinson has in the last hour confessed to the murder of Amy Graham.'

'Good work, Kevin. You and the team have worked wonders on this.'

'Thank you, sir, I wonder if I can come over tomorrow morning and have a chat with you.'

'Yes of course, I'm free until ten o'clock. Is there something else I should know about?'

'It's a bit complicated sir, nothing to do with the Amy Graham case, I'll see you just after nine.'

Kevin replaced the phone, he knew his work now was far from over.

Chapter 20

Cheshire Police HQ
Tuesday, 27th March 2001, 9am

DCI Maxfield decided he needed to speak personally with the ACC Crime regarding the DNA situation. It was far too delicate a matter to discuss with the rest of the investigation team so as arranged he decided to drive over to Chester HQ for the early morning meeting with Ian Mossley.

'Come in Kevin, it's good to see you and congratulations again on the DNA mass screening, I'll say this it certainly got the result we were after.

'Well, we've also got another DNA match sir against two closed cases!'

'Even better, that's great news.'

'But it goes back to the sixties.'

'What! how on earth has that happened?'

'It's like this sir when we moved from Holmes1 to Holmes2 in the late 90s the force hit a bit of a quiet patch on investigations so one of our senior CID officers here at HQ decided to open up some of the cold cases for further investigation, they back record converted the cards onto Holmes2 and at the same time captured any DNA and forensic evidence attached to those cases. This other DNA match apparently came from both an envelope of a letter that was sent into the incident room at the time together with swabs taken at the time from one of the bodies. We've also got a match with one of the young lads who gave us a DNA sample.'

'You are joking, but he can't be more than twenty-one years of age?'

'Yes, but it's a familial DNA match, it links back to his family, but that's not the real problem sir!'

Kevin Maxfield hesitated, 'I don't really know how to best put this…'

'Well, come on, spit it out Kevin, what is it?'

'I'm sorry it's a bit delicate sir!'

'What is it?'

'You won't believe this but the young lad is Jason Ellis!'

Chapter 21

Congleton Police Station
Wednesday, 28th March 2001, 9.30pm

The ACC Crime and DCI Maxfield had been deep in discussion the previous evening on how best to deal with the closed cases from 1967. It was agreed that because of the sensitivity of the DNA match with these two cases that only the DCI and DS Wood should get completely familiar with them before making their next move. They had agreed that in no circumstances should the DNA match on the two closed cases be discussed with any other force members. The DCI handed over the SIO role on the Amy Graham case to DI Hinckley whilst he worked with DS Wood on the cold cases in a locked office at Congleton. They were working late into the night on the linked cases.

Fortunately, both of the cold cases had been migrated to Holmes together with full briefing reports should the cases get re-opened later and it didn't take the two officers long to familiarise themselves.

'Certainly better than wading through all those old cards they used to use on the manual system boss,' said DS Wood, 'it would have taken us months to get up to speed on these.'

'Agreed, it's a bit before my time John. How are you getting on tracing the family connections in North Wales?'

'Pretty good actually, I think we are almost ready for a day trip to the seaside boss.'

Chapter 22

Menai Bridge, Anglesea
Friday, 30th March 2001, 1.30pm

DCI Maxfield and DS Wood drove across to North Wales. The A55 was quiet and they were well ahead of schedule for their meeting at Menai Bridge. They even had time to stop for a coffee break en-route just outside Colwyn Bay.

As they crossed the straits onto the island of Anglesey the DCI remarked how he used to visit the island when as a child.

'We had some wonderful holidays over here John, camping over at Benllech and playing on the sands down at Red Wharf Bay. This has certainly brought back memories.'

They turned right over the bridge and soon found the gravel driveway leading to the rest home. As they turned the corner there in front of them was what had once been a grand manor house now covered in ivy which could easily be mistaken for a five-star hotel.

'Well, this looks like the place, I wasn't sure what to expect to be honest but I imagine this costs a bob or two per week,' said the DCI as they parked in the visitors' car park.

'I wouldn't mind a week or two here myself,' remarked DS Wood as they made their way down the curved pathway to the impressive entrance hall.

'Not sure the police pension would cover that,' laughed the DCI, 'but wow just take a look back there, what a view!'

They turned around and across the manicured lawns, the most wonderful view of the Menai straits below them with small fishing boats anchored up in the bay. In the distance they could clearly see the Snowdonia mountain range rising majestically above the scene.

The two detectives entered from the outer hallway to a large reception area and strolled up to the large oak desk.

Ever observant the DCI couldn't help noticing the receptionists name badge as they approached the desk.

'Oh, good afternoon Mrs Morris, my name is DCI Maxfield and this is DS Wood, I wonder if it's possible for us to see Mr Keith Ellis?' he said showing his warrant card.

For a second Mrs Morris wondered how the DCI knew her name.

'Yes of course, he's in our Gladstone lounge suite just next to the restaurant. Could you please sign the visitors' book and I'll take you through to him.'

Both officers signed the book as Mrs Morris handed them a visitor's badge each.

'Actually, is it possible to see him in a private room?' enquired the DCI, 'It's personal I'm afraid and we don't wish to disturb your other residents with our conversation.'

'Yes of course, if you'd like to go through to the small meeting room that's just across the corridor there and I'll bring him over. He should have finished his lunch by now.'

The two detectives made their way across into the adjoining meeting room which was set out with six chairs and a large oval table. On the walls were various award certificates and three spectacular paintings of the Menai Straits showing different times of the day.

Five minutes later Mrs Morris arrived back escorting an old grey-haired man who was walking with the aid of a walking stick. He must have been in his late seventies, possibly early eighties, tanned and smartly dressed in chinos, brown shoes and an open necked blue checked shirt.

'These are the two gentlemen to see you Mr Ellis. I'll leave you with them. Just call me if you need anything, I'll just be outside in reception.'

'Mr Ellis, my name is DCI Maxfield and this is DS Wood, we need to speak to you about two separate incidents that happened in Saughall and Chester back in 1967.'

'That's a long time ago and my memory isn't as good as it was in those days,' sighed Keith Ellis, 'but all I can say is it's taken you long enough.'

'Pardon!' exclaimed the DCI who was completely taken aback by the remarks.

'It's about Jennifer and Anne isn't it. Well, I've lived with this for decades, every time I've seen a police car or heard a siren, I thought that's it, the games up. But of course, it's not a game is it, yes, I did it. I killed both those girls, I'm ashamed of it now but at the time I couldn't see any way out of the situation.'

DCI Maxfield couldn't believe his ears.

'What situation are we talking about Mr Ellis?' said the DCI leaving DS Wood to make any notes.

'As you probably know by now, I was married to Jennifer's mother Nancy, god rest her soul. Nancy died about ten years ago, she never got over Jennifer's death. Of course I never told her what had happened that night although I think she had an inkling. Jennifer came to stop with us one weekend in Beaumaris, we went out for a meal and had a few drinks. We were having a lovely time the three of us and somehow whether it was the drink but I thought Jennifer was coming on to me. She was a lovely girl and to be honest I fancied her like mad. I became obsessed with the idea of having an affair with her, I knew it was wrong but this voice inside my head drove me on. I couldn't stop thinking about her. Anyway, one night when I was supposed to be working, I drove up to Chester, I knew where she worked in that night club. I had a few drinks there and I made a pass at her, she went berserk embarrassing me in front of everyone. I returned to Beaumaris and a week or two later I tried again, she threatened this time to tell her mum and told me that she had already told her friend Anne. I can't remember her surname.'

'That would be Anne Barlow?'

'Yes, that's right, she was a stunner as well. Any way it had all got out of hand and one night I decided to get my own back. Stupid now when I think about it. I waited for my moment and went back to Chester and I guess you know the rest. I took her to that old run down cottage not far from Saughall. I'd found that by accident when I was looking in an estate agent's window, it seemed the perfect location and I managed to break into the place. The foot and mouth fires at the time gave me the perfect opportunity to get rid of the body and all was going to plan until I was disturbed by someone and I had to wait until the middle of the night before finally disposing of her.'

'I panicked a day or two after and went back to the old derelict cottage to tidy up, I wasn't sure I'd left any evidence there you see.'

'But what about Anne Barlow, how was she involved in all this, what happened there?' piped up DS Wood.

'Well, I knew that Jennifer had confided with Anne, she had told me that herself. A few days after Jennifer went missing, I got a phone call from Anne, she wanted to speak to Nancy. I knew what that was all about and told her Nancy wasn't there. From that moment on I knew I had to also get rid of Anne so I waited for the right opportunity. Anne thought Jennifer had gone away somewhere. Anyway, with Anne, I watched her every move, I even knew where she had moved to in Shotton. Then I broke into her bedsit and waited for her one night. She put up a fight mind you, she was strong. I had plans to drop her body in the River Dee but again someone spotted my car. I had to think fast and decided to leave the body in that old boatshed.'

'And you kept a shoe as a souvenir?'

'Oh, that yes, I've always had a thing about ladies' shoes, it's a weakness of mine, always has been. Can I ask how you eventually found me?'

'Well, without going into detail, be careful who you write to!'

Up until this point Keith Ellis had been calm and related the events of his story in 1967 without any emotion whatsoever. Then suddenly without any warning he buried his head in his hands and wept uncontrollably.

DCI Maxfield waited for the crying to subside.

'Keith Ellis, I'm arresting you for the murders of Jennifer Webb and Anne Barlow. You do not have to say anything, but it may harm your defence, if you do not mention when questioned something which you later rely on in court.

Anything you do say may be given as evidence. Do you understand?'

'Yes, I do.'

Some thirty minutes later the DCI and DS were driving back to Chester down the A55 but this time accompanying their new passenger – Keith Ellis.

Chapter 23

Cheshire Police HQ – Chief Constables Office
Friday, 30th March 2001, 6.00pm

Sorry to disturb you chief but the ACC Crime and DCI Maxfield would like to see you as a matter of urgency. They are waiting outside, shall I send them in?' said Beryl King the chief's PA as she placed the tray of teapot, cup and saucer on his desk.

'Well, I was really hoping for an early finish tonight but yes, if it's urgent, then please show them in Beryl,' replied the chief who was busy finishing a Police Authority report that he was working on.

'Come in, good evening gentlemen and also congratulations Kevin on getting a result on that latest murder case at Congleton. Well done, good work.'

'Thank you, sir, it was teamwork after all.'

'Good, I'm sure it was, so how can I be of help, I imagine this is something to do with that case?'

'Yes and no sir, but I'll let Kevin explain the situation,' replied the ACC.

'Well sir, it's a bit delicate this but as you know we ran a DNA mass screening process in Congleton?'

'Yes, very costly but at least it got the results,' replied the chief as he took a sip of tea.

'The DNA matching process brought out more than we had expected sir. It also through a familial DNA check found matches with two other closed cases.'

'Splendid, it gets even better. A good investment and great use of technology.'

'Well sir, through this we have this afternoon arrested a man over in Anglesey for the murders of Jennifer Webb and Anne Barlow. These murders go back to 1967.'

'Excellent, I'm not familiar with the cases but well done I'm impressed, it gets even better.'

'Well sir, the DNA match in Congleton came from your own son Jason and the man we arrested whose name is Keith Ellis, is in fact his grandad, your father sir!'

Epilogue

A man in his late 70s has been charged with murdering his step-daughter and her friend in 1967. Keith Ellis aged 78 from Menai Bridge, Anglesey has been charged with murdering Jennifer Webb and her friend Anne Barlow and has been remanded in custody to appear at Chester Magistrates Court this morning.

A young man has been charged with the murder of his girlfriend in Congleton, Cheshire in February 2001. Cameron Wilkinson aged 20 from Congleton, Cheshire has been charged with murdering Amy Graham and has been remanded in custody to appear at Macclesfield Magistrates Court this morning.

Glossary of Terms

In writing this crime novel, I have tried wherever possible to avoid using Police acronyms; however, sometimes I have felt the need to include them.

CPS – Crown Prosecution Service

Dispatchers – The Control room staff responsible for dispatching resources to a particular scene

HOLMES – The UK major incident computer system (Home Office Large Major Enquiry System)

MG Forms – The Manual of Guidance series of forms to provide standard procedures and forms for prosecution files across a number of agencies

Mispers – Missing Persons

Nominals – The index records normally relating to offenders, suspects etc but in some systems can also include witnesses and persons of interest.

SIO – Senior Investigating Officer

SOCO – Scenes of Crime Officers